OCCULT ASSASSIN
Damnation Code
Book 1

WILLIAM MASSA

CHAPTER ONE

THE BLADE PRESSED against Steve Delaney's neck, drawing a line of blood. He swallowed hard, tasting the salty beads of perspiration trickling down his face. How the hell had he gotten himself into this terrible ordeal?

His day had started off innocently enough. After a leisurely breakfast of bacon, eggs and toast, he found himself behind the wheel of his Toyota Camry cruising the sloping, bustling streets of San Francisco.

In his old life as a restaurant manager his schedule was dominated by a soul-deadening seventy-hour workweek. Stress defined his life. Nowadays, as an *EasyRides* driver, Steve made his own hours and worked only when he wanted to. There were bills to be paid — God, they never seemed to stop — but at least he wasn't a slave to his job anymore. The successful professionals among his friends all frowned at his latest career move and hoped that it would turn out to be a case of temporary insanity. To hell with them! Steve was enjoying the freedom and peace of mind that came with his new occupation.

Steve's dash-mounted iPhone, which was running Google Maps, lit up. A pin flashed onscreen, indicating the location of a nearby rider. Immediately a countdown kicked in. Being the driver closest to the potential fare, Steve had exactly fifteen seconds to accept the ride or it would be assigned to another driver.

He tapped the ACCEPT button and twisted the wheel, heading east on the next street. A few minutes later, Steve slowed to a cruise and scoped the sidewalk for his pickup. When he reached the address given, he pushed the ARRIVE tab. This would signal to his rider to be on the lookout for his car.

A woman in her mid-twenties suddenly strode up to his vehicle. She wore jeans, a blazer and geek chic glasses. Steve figured her for an employee of one of the many tech-sector upstarts in the Bay Area. Her look seemed carefully designed to downplay her sensuality. *With the right dress and makeup, though, this gal would be a real looker*, he thought.

Steve flashed the lady a big smile as she got in the car. "Evening. How are you tonight?"

"Good, thank you."

"Lean back and enjoy the ride. If you're thirsty or hungry, help yourself to a bottle of water and an energy bar."

Refreshments lined the back of the car. They went a long way in winning those all-important favorable reviews from his customers. Good reviews led to more work and in turn, more dollars in his pocket. Managing a restaurant had taught him a thing or two about the importance of online feedback in the Digital Age.

The woman closed the door. Steve floored the gas. According to the destination on his app, they were headed to Fisherman's Wharf. Turning down Lombard Street, Steve continued to study his passenger in the rearview mirror. Like everyone else in this town, she seemed married to her smartphone and oblivious to her surroundings.

Upon closer inspection his initial impression stood confirmed — under the geek-girl veneer was a real hottie. Unfortunately, she didn't seem like the chatty type, unless you counted instant messages. Steve searched his mind for a funny icebreaker but lacking inspiration, he decided to concentrate on traffic.

They soon reached the top of Russian Hill and turned left onto Hyde. Fort Mason, Aquatic Park and Alcatraz Island stretched out before them, offering a panoramic view spanning from the Golden Gate to the Embarcadero.

Just ahead, a cable car clanged its way down the hill. Steve adjusted his speed and followed the rumbling tram at a safe distance. Tourists dangled camera-phones from their seats in the trolley, marveling at the stunning view while taking pics. Steve didn't blame them. No matter how many times he took this final plunge down the hilly Hyde Street to the Bay, it never got old. Once again he thanked the lucky stars that had steered him away from his old job.

His good mood came to an abrupt end when he felt fingers grab his hair and violently pull his head back. Cold metal bit into his throat. A terrified glance in the mirror revealed a hunting knife pressed against his bobbing Adam's apple.

Oh my God... this can't be happening...

"Keep driving," the woman hissed. "Don't do anything stupid."

Fighting back his mounting terror, Steve did as instructed, his hands clammy despite the air conditioner.

"What are you doing?" he croaked.

"Shut the fuck up and keep your eyes on the road."

She dug the razor-sharp point into his neck, drawing a thin line of blood.

"Lady, I don't carry any money on me," he stammered.

"I said to keep your fucking mouth shut!"

This time the knife's edge cut deeper and Steve received the message loud and clear. It took every ounce of self-control to keep his mind on the flow of traffic. What did this psycho bitch want from him?

"Do exactly as I say and you'll be okay. Do you understand?"

"Yes."

"Now lean forward and replace the phone on your dash with mine. Make sure the camera is pointing directly at you. Nod if you understand."

Steve nodded once more. Like an automaton, he

swapped the phones on his dashboard with one hand while the other steered the car. If he lost control of the wheel, he knew his last sensation would be the bite of the blade sawing through the soft meat of his throat.

Steve's horrified features flickered onto the screen of the newly mounted iPhone. The camera was on, recording his fear.

"What are you going to do?" he asked the knife-wielding passenger.

"Did I give you permission to talk?"

The blade dug deeper and Steve bit his tongue before letting another sound escape from his lips. The image on the phone split into two smaller screens. The faces of another man and a woman appeared. Their circumstances were identical to his own. Behind them, someone's hand pressed a knife to each of their jugular veins. Steve saw his terror mirrored in their haunted gazes.

Who were these people? This stuff happened in movies but not in the real world.

A fourth person joined the video call. The newcomer wasn't another victim but appeared to be the mastermind behind the nightmare. He wore a robotic death mask straight out of some apocalyptic sci-fi horror film. A tangled web of transistors, cables and circuits pockmarked the mask's texture like cybernetic acne. The figure's bass rumbling, electronically distorted voice boomed through the moving car, reciting words in an ancient, alien tongue.

For a frozen moment, the victims onscreen

exchanged haunted glances. *They must be seeing me on their own screens,* Steve thought. Then the knives drew their blade-edges across the other drivers' throats.

Steve's eyes widened as pulsating heat washed down his neck. His hands went for his gushing throat in a desperate attempt to quell the bleeding.

The other victims fought similarly hopeless battles on the phone's screen. Tortured death rattles resounded through the Camry, underscored by the masked man's singsong chant. This had turned into a videoconference from hell.

Steve's foot grew heavy and mashed the gas. The Camry hurtled forward, out of control now. The car caught up with the trolley and crumpled into its back end with a ferocious shriek of twisted metal and panicked tourists. A couple of hapless cable-car riders lost their grip and were sent flying like ragdolls.

Smoke and steam plumed from the contorted hood of the Camry. Pitiful screams pierced the air and the stench of burning oil became overpowering. Steve's head slumped against the steering wheel, his shirt and jeans drenched a dark scarlet. His dying, crimson-spattered face stared back at him from the cellphone mounted on his dash.

While his life poured out in a stream of red, a hand reached from the back of the car to collect her mobile. There was a metallic snap as the passenger unfastened her seat belt, followed by the screech of a car door being kicked open.

Steve shifted his dimming gaze, lips bubbling crimson, the people outside his spiderwebbed windshield now reduced to blurry outlines. Like ghosts they hovered in his fading field of vision until the darkness consumed them and the world turned black.

***

Less than an hour later, Steve Delaney's murderer arrived at the Golden Gate Bridge. Head held high, her gait steady and purposeful, she crossed the majestic red bridge until she reached its center.

She tilted her head toward the railing, gusts of wind buffeting her hair. Cars whipped by, a pulsing flow of traffic between San Francisco and Oakland.

Soon two men joined her. They were dressed more casually — jeans, flannel shirts and Converse sneakers — but their blank expressions mirrored her own. One other damning detail linked these three individuals. Each carried a blade caked with a dead person's blood. They'd made the sacrifice required of them but one final offering remained to prove their devotion.

Without even trading glances, the three killers scaled the steel railing together, their movements eerily synchronized. Before anyone could stop them, the trio had vanished from view, plunging to their deaths in the Bay below.

CHAPTER TWO

THE ROAR OF gunfire split the air and echoed across the arid Afghan mountain. Two members of the twelve-man team of special operators went down in a mist of red as Kalashnikovs unleashed a ribbon of lead.

It's a trap, Mark Talon thought.

Instincts overruling fear, the Delta Force operator returned fire. Fueled by a burst of adrenaline, he bolted toward the ridgeline with his MP4 blazing. There was no distinction between himself and the weapon in his gloved hand; they had fused to become one deadly organism programmed to take out the enemy hiding in the steeper hills overlooking the pass. Sweat masked his face and his boots crunched over the rocky terrain. The white noise of incessant popping and hissing accompanied his ascent.

Like everyone on the team Talon was dressed like an Afghan, sporting the traditional local garb. The Taliban wasn't fooled. They knew that under the facial hair and headdresses were American soldiers. Someone had tipped them off.

Talon cursed. He hadn't quite trusted the

guerilla leader-turned-informant when the man told them that Taliban fighters would use this pass to smuggle guns over the Pakistan border. Then again, it was hard to trust anyone in a country torn apart by war. Sometimes you had to take a gamble and hope it worked out. This time the risk had backfired and instead of catching the terrorists in the act, they'd walked into a goddamn ambush.

Making matters worse, they were babysitting some hotshot reporter who'd been embedded with the unit for the last eight days. Why couldn't the politicians understand that a "shadow war" meant operating in the shadows? Cameras and journalists weren't an option. No matter how attractive or charming they might be.

Michelle Rossi had turned into quite a distraction to everyone, including himself. A dead civilian wouldn't go over well with the brass but if Talon was to be honest, his concern for the brunette journalist ran a bit deeper. He was embarrassed to admit it, but he was starting to like the reporter. Her safety was the first thing on his mind.

Three feet from Talon's position a grenade tore up the ground. The six-foot tall, sinewy operator instinctively dove forward. The impact of hitting the gravel sent a jolt through his entire body, but the armor under his robe absorbed the brunt of it.

As he tugged down the scarf covering his face, heavy wool scratching his newly grown beard, Talon scoped the dark rocks that loomed ahead. Death was waiting in those outcroppings. How many good soldiers had the enemy already claimed?

Talon vowed not to be one of them as he scanned the rocks for the human-shaped shadows raining lead on his team. Responding to a flicker of movement, he squeezed the trigger of his weapon and a Taliban fighter collapsed in a string-cut sprawl. Another quick burst cut down the man with the grenade launcher hiding near him.

Two down.

Lead ravaged the hillside as Talon's radio crackled and the voice of Sergeant Erik Garrison, his unit's commanding officer, filled his ear. "Charlie Four, this is Charlie Six, air support is a no-go..."

Erik's voice was drowned out as a mortar ignited ten feet from Talon's position. Heat singed the air and shrapnel showered down on him.

He needed to move.

With that in mind Talon sprang to his feet, his bullets carving a path for him as he sprinted toward the next boulder. He distinctly made out screams. A moment later, the enemy fire stopped.

Face pressed against the cold rock, he listened. The pass had grown silent and for one illogical second he was convinced he was the only man left standing. Couldn't be. He stole a look back but there was no sign of the team.

No sign of Michelle.

Fear rippled up his spine. Immediately he crushed the emotion before it could infect his brain and paralyze him. There a perfectly logical reason for the quiet. The others were getting their bearings behind some rock, the same way he was.

Eyes alert, body coiled, Talon continued his advance up the hillside. He was heading for a string of boulders that lined the mountain like jagged stone teeth. To his surprise, the shelling didn't resume. Could he have hit them all?

Staying low to offer his enemies less of a target, Talon circled the boulders and froze. Splayed out before him were the bloodied bodies of the combatants he'd taken out. But something was wrong. Terribly wrong.

These faces didn't belong to the enemy. These were Americans.

His team members.

What have I done?

The arm of one of the dead soldiers shot out at him and clawed his leg, mouth gurgling blood.

A scream exploded from Talon's lips…

***

Talon's eyes snapped open and he was hit with a flash of blinding light. Blinking away his confusion, he realized that the passenger sitting next to him had leaned over and raised the shade of the airplane window. Judging from the flashing signs and the airport jumping into view outside the window, the plane had begun its descent to San Francisco International Airport.

Clearly, the kid didn't want to miss one second of the spectacle. "Sorry," he muttered sheepishly.

"No worries," Talon said. He was relieved to be

awake after the nightmare. Swallowing hard, Talon wiped the beads of perspiration from his face and wished the flight attendants were still serving drinks.

The image of his lifeless team members still tormented him during the plane's descent. The ambush they'd walked into two years ago had unfolded a bit differently in real life. There were no casualties from friendly fire, but the encounter had cost three good men their lives.

Ironically enough, the attack had also brought him and Michelle closer, paving the way for their eventual romance. She was the reason why he'd taken a two-week vacation from his military duties. He was here to pay her a surprise visit in her hometown of San Francisco.

Heavy landing gears crunched against the runway and their vibrations rattled the plane, jolting Talon from his thoughts.

As the jet taxied to its terminal, he turned on his phone. Five text messages were waiting for him. Michelle didn't know about his visit but his old superior officer, Erik Garrison, did.

Erik lived in Oakland now; he resigned from active duty exactly a month after the ambush. It was Erik who'd made the call to trust the guerilla leader and lead his men into a kill-zone. He blamed himself for the three casualties involved and remained unwilling to forgive himself. There was no way Erik could've known what was coming, but it didn't change the man's feelings. He began a downward spiral fueled by alcohol and drugs. Since taking early retirement he'd been living on a meager disability pension and thus far had failed to put the broken pieces of his life back together.

Talon knew his friend was in a dark place and worried about him. It was hard enough to adjust to civilian life without being haunted by guilt. Suicide rates were at an all-time high among veterans, and Erik had indicated on numerous occasions that he was thinking of eating a bullet. Talon planned to drop by Erik's place in the coming days. Hopefully, seeing a familiar face might help a little.

With that plan in mind, he snatched his duffle bag from the overhead compartment. Next to him, an elderly lady struggled with her bag. "Let me help you with that," Talon said.

His strong hand closed around the handle of the monstrous suitcase. Holy shit, how did Granny manage to drag this beast onto the plane? "Here you go, ma'am."

The lady's eyes lit up with gratitude and she smiled at her rescuer. "Thank you so much, so kind of you."

Talon offered to carry the suitcase until they located a cart in the terminal. The airport was abuzz with activity. A number of flights had landed within minutes of each other and tired, frustrated travelers oozed stress as they fought through rings of people to claim their luggage.

"Is someone picking you up, or will you be hailing a cab?" Talon asked his new friend, who had introduced herself as Mrs. Cane.

"My daughter is supposed to be waiting for me—"

"Mom!"

An attractive blonde in her mid-twenties rapidly approached Mrs. Cane. The elderly lady winked at Talon in a conspiratorial manner.

Someone is trying to play matchmaker, Talon thought.

There was immediate interest in the daughter's eyes. Talon's gray shirt and faded brown leather jacket did little to hide his lean but muscular frame. As a member of 1st Special Forces Operational Detachment-Delta, Sgt. Talon was in peak physical condition. His swarthy good looks and easy smile didn't hurt either. Most people wouldn't have taken him for an elite soldier, with his longish hair and beard, but special-ops soldiers followed more relaxed grooming standards than rank-and-file military personnel.

While Mrs. Cane's daughter was quite lovely, Talon only had eyes for the reporter who'd stolen his heart two year earlier, in Afghanistan. "I see you found your ride. You two have a great day now."

Waving goodbye, he merged with the crowd of travelers surging toward the nearest exit. His years of military service had taught Talon to be a minimalist and restrict his luggage to one carry-on bag, and he was able to bypass the crowds.

He stepped through the automatic doors and reached the adjoining sidewalk. The air outside was hot and thick but felt like a fresh breeze compared to Afghanistan's arid, blistering desert temperatures.

It's good to be back in the States.

Talon scanned the cabstand and decided to skip

the long line. The train station was only a short walk from the United Airlines terminal.

Soon he was seated on the BART as it rattled toward San Francisco. The airport receded in the distance and residential sprawl took over.

Once again his mind turned to Michelle. He couldn't stop thinking about her. Those mysterious brown eyes flecked with green. That lush auburn hair and perfect olive complexion. The delicate line of her neck.

There was no way around it — Talon had fallen hard for the journalist. Despite his initial misgiving about her presence with the unit, he'd quickly realized that Michelle wasn't what he expected.

With her looks and brains she could've pursued any number of glamorous careers, but she chose to risk her life in the mountains with him and his men. When he brought this up to her, Michelle merely smiled wearily and said that certain stories needed to be told, and certain voices needed to be heard.

Michelle remained embedded for six more days after the ambush and she proved to have a transformative effect on Talon. He'd mastered the art of disconnecting from the violence and misery that he encountered on a daily basis. Michelle, on the other hand, allowed herself to emotionally respond to the horrors unfolding around her. Her ability to show vulnerability had pierced Talon's iron guard and reminded him that there was a human heart beating under his own armor.

It was okay to feel.

To give a damn.

In fact, it was necessary, if he didn't want to end up in the psych ward of some V.A. hospital down the line. He didn't need to sacrifice his humanity and become a machine to be an effective warrior.

While they bonded during her time with the unit, most likely their relationship wouldn't have gone further. But fate seemed to smile upon them. Their paths crossed again in Dubai, when Talon was catching up on some much-needed R&R. Sparks flew and the rest was history.

Two years later, they now saw each other as often as their demanding careers permitted.

Talon had dated his fair share of women over the years, but the nature of his grueling work made it difficult for him to get serious with anyone. He could be activated at a moment's notice and wind up halfway across the globe, in some warzone.

It took a certain kind of woman to put up with the reality of his profession.

A woman like Michelle Rossi.

He touched the ring case in his pocket and took a deep breath. Michelle didn't know he was coming to San Francisco for a surprise visit, let alone that he was here to propose.

Talon wasn't a man prone to nervousness. A decade in the military — five years in the regular Army and then another five in Special Forces — had imbued him with steely discipline and control over his emotions. Danger actually sharpened his focus. Jumping out of airplanes, crossing minefields or battling terrorists was all in a day's work. Proposing to his girlfriend; now there was something that made him work up a nervous sweat.

The train pulled into the city. Talon got off at the next stop and headed for the offices of the *San Francisco Chronicle*. He spotted a flower shop on the way and decided to pick up a bouquet for his sweetheart. No way he'd show up at his girl's office empty-handed.

Once inside the store, Talon concluded within seconds that the owner was Persian. Based on his age, the man was probably a refugee from the Iranian Revolution who had come to the States in the '70s.

Talon addressed the man in near-perfect Farsi. "I need flowers for the love of my life. Can you help me out? I barely know the difference between a rose and a tulip."

The florist beamed, charmed by Talon's ability to speak to him in his native language. In lightly accented English, he said, "My friend, I'll make something real nice for you and your sweetheart."

With a magician's skill, the Persian went to work. Talon followed the man's quick-moving fingers as they snatched flowers from an assortment of vases. In a matter of seconds he'd produced an arrangement that looked pretty damn impressive, even to Talon's botanically challenged brain.

"Thanks, she'll love these," Talon said. He paid the Persian and continued on his way. He made another quick stop at a local grocery store and purchased a bottle of wine, a few fancy cheeses and crackers, grapes and some delicious-looking Tiramisu. The plan was to take Michelle on a romantic picnic in Dolores Park, and pop the question before he lost his nerve. He wanted it to be memorable but not overblown, romantic but not saccharine.

A rush of anticipation fueled his stride as he walked those last few blocks toward Fifth and Mission. He still sported a grin when he stepped through the main entrance of the *San Francisco Chronicle.* Other businesses had moved into the newspaper's building. Workers clad in tech-upstart chic shuttled between sparkling water dispensers and rows of Apple computers.

The newspaper was becoming increasingly isolated in a building they had occupied since 1924. It was a reminder how the economics of news had changed since the dawn of the Internet. According to Michelle, rumors of a move made the rounds as frequently as wacky news tips about the Zodiac.

Talon entered the front lobby of the *Chronicle* and winked conspiratorially at the receptionist, signaling that he didn't want her to ruin his surprise visit. This was going to be good. The pressure of the impending proposal was gone, replaced with growing excitement.

While crossing the bustling bullpen, he noticed the rugged, worn appearance of the cubicles, and how they formed a sharp contrast to the sleek office space he'd glimpsed on the other floor. The *Chronicle* wasn't some well-funded technology enterprise but an old-media bastion struggling to stay afloat in an ever-changing media landscape.

He homed in on Michelle's desk. The moment he spotted her, a warm feeling filled his heart. She was scrunched in her Aeron chair, hair pulled back in a tight ponytail and serious eyes riveted to her computer monitor. She was wearing a pair of headphones and talking to a woman on the computer.

Talon's last two months had been defined by the hardship of war. Seeing the woman he loved made the dark moments grow distant in his memory and gave him hope for the future.

Michelle. His girl and, hopefully, soon his wife...

If he should be so lucky.

Sensing his approach, Michelle looked up and their eyes met. She stifled her whoop of joy and told the woman she was Skyping with to hold on for a sec. She tore off her ear-buds and rushed to Talon. Their arms and their lips quickly interlocked. All thoughts took a backseat to the intensity of their fierce embrace. His world reduced to the feel of Michelle's soft skin, the taste of her breath, and the gentle tickle of her hair. He breathed in her intoxicating scent.

Michelle was the one who applied the brakes to their building passion, realizing she was still at work. She took a step back and caught half the news office looking away and pretending to be busy with their jobs.

Talon grinned sheepishly. "Maybe I should've given you a heads up..."

"Maybe we just need to get out of here and find

a more private place to celebrate."

"Sounds good. Oh, by the way, these are for you."

Michelle beamed when Talon handed her the Iranian's lovely floral arrangement. "Mark, they're beautiful! Thank you, darling." She pressed the petals close to her cheek.

"Let me just wrap up this call and we'll be on our way," Michelle said as she turned back to her workstation and donned her headphones again.

Talon circled Michelle's desk to gain a visual on the person she was chatting with. Anxiety marred the young woman's attractive features, her nervous tension palpable. Talon couldn't quite make out their conversation.

The screen went dark and Michelle turned toward him. There was a trace of concern in her eyes, but she quickly cast it aside. "All ready. Let's blow this joint."

As they headed down the stairs, Talon asked, "What was that all about?"

"Just one of my sources."

"Cooking up some big new story?"

"Always."

Talon waited for more but Michelle remained mum on the matter. She could be a bit secretive about her work, especially in those crucial early stages when she was still compiling research. Discretion was something else they shared in common.

Michelle leaned closer and kissed him again and all thoughts of the Skype conversation evaporated. "Hmmm, you smell good for a guy who crawls in the dirt for a living."

Talon smiled and held up his grocery bag.

"Feeling up for lunch in the park?"

"Hmm, you make it hard for a girl to say no."

Hand-in-hand, they stepped out of the building, trailed by both envious and curious glances. The two of them shared something pretty special and someone would have to be blind not to pick up on it.

Less than an hour later, they were making out in Dolores Park, their hands roaming and exploring as they lay under a tree in the grass. They had barely touched the crackers and cheese. Most of the wine remained in the plastic cups Talon had brought along for the occasion. Anyone passing by would have taken them for a couple of love-struck teenagers.

"It might be time to get a room," Michelle joked as she caught her breath.

Talon nodded a little too fast. He couldn't wait to 'get a room' but there was something else that he needed to do first. Misinterpreting his hesitation, Michelle caressed the stubble on his face. "Is everything okay, babe? If there's something you need to talk about…"

Michelle was all too aware of the challenges men like Talon faced. The horrors they confronted on a daily basis. He eyed her deeply and knew the moment had come to be a man. His throat felt dry as spoke. "I brought you here because a) I'm a romantic softie and b) there's something I want to ask you."

He refilled Michelle's cup with wine and suddenly his hands were shaking. Man, he was acting like some high-school kid out on a first date.

"I know, wine in a plastic cup, ain't I a classy guy?"

"Probably a step up from eating the nasty parts of goats to impress village elders," Michelle teased.

"Don't knock Afghani cuisine. It'll catch on."

Michelle grinned as she sipped her wine.

Talon had rehearsed his speech for days now, racking his brain for the perfect words. He nervously downed his entire cup of wine and Michelle shot him a surprised look. "You all right?"

Talon knelt before her in the grass. "You might want to get up for this next part."

"Oh my God..." Realization filled her eyes and Talon knew there was no turning back now. He fumbled getting the ring box out of his pocket. Last time he'd felt this nervous was when he'd foolishly decided to take a role in a high school play. Shakespeare wasn't his friend.

"Michelle, two years ago I wasn't happy when I learned some reporter was supposed to spend eight days with my unit. A week later I was a different man playing a different tune."

This is so cheesy. His Delta buddies would be laughing their asses off if they could hear him now. It had sounded good in his mind but spoken out loud... Screw it! He was putting it all out there. He meant every word he said and was expressing himself as best he could. He'd never claimed to be a poet.

Tears welled in Michelle's eyes as he continued. "The last two years have been the happiest years of my life, despite some of the worst combat I've had to endure. Knowing that you're in my life, Michelle, reminds me what I'm fighting for."

Talon took a deep breath and opened the ring case. He'd purchased the ring — a three-diamond in 15K white gold — in New York City's jewelry district. An old Army buddy turned jeweler helped him pick out something tasteful and beautiful. It was only right that the woman who'd transformed his world receive a ring worthy of her.

Michelle was both sobbing and giggling now. Talon never got a chance to actually mouth his proposal as she engulfed him in a bear hug. Her kisses and tears spoke louder than words.

Talon's heart beat with joy as they headed to Michelle's rent-controlled townhouse in Mission Bay. The moment they stepped into her place, Talon attacked her and they hit the carpet. Within seconds the clothes had come off in a heady, fumbling rush of animal passion and pent-up emotion. They both shook as they climaxed, soaked in perspiration.

They laid on the floor, hands and bodies entwined. The problems of the world seemed a million miles away. The blood and dust of the wars Talon was fighting belonged to another reality.

There was only Michelle and himself. Their bodies. Their passion. Their love.

They were still recuperating from their

lovemaking, sipping beer and snacking on chips when Talon's phone buzzed.

Damn it!

He ignored the call, but whoever was trying to reach him refused to take no for an answer. After the fourth call, his cell vibrated with two incoming text messages. Someone desperately needed to get in touch with him. Not tomorrow, or in an hour, but *right now.* Cursing under his breath, he pulled away from Michelle.

"I'm sorry..." He scanned the phone and his face fell.

"Is it Erik?" Michelle asked with concern. She remembered the sergeant all too well.

Talon nodded. Michelle's lipstick and mascara were smeared, her hair tangled. *God, she's beautiful,* he thought.

"He needs your help, doesn't he?"

Damn! Talk about perfect timing!

Judging from the slurred, rambling voicemail and incoherent texts, Erik was having a bad night.

"He sounds like he's in bad shape," Talon said.

"You think he might hurt himself?"

Talon shrugged. The Erik he'd served with was a force of nature, a man whose will to fight burned with the intensity of a bright star in its prime. This new Erik was a pale shadow of that man.

"You should go to him," Michelle said.

Talon's face fell and Michelle cupped his rugged features in her hands. "If something should happen to him, you'll never forgive yourself."

Michelle's selfless words reminded Talon why

he loved her so much. He rose reluctantly and sent Erik a quick text to say that he was on his way. He kissed Michelle and it lingered, almost reigniting their passion. Michelle gently pulled away. "Go help your friend."

She handed him her car keys. "I'm parked about five cars down the block. I'll be here waiting for you when you come back."

Talon gave her an earnest look and said, "Love you."

Her smile always knocked his socks off. "I love you too."

Once outside, his eyes probed the dark road and spotted Michelle's car — a red Nissan. The keys jingled in his hand as he walked down the abandoned sidewalk.

Talon got into the Nissan and slid into traffic. He never noticed the black van with tinted windows, parked across the street from Michelle's place. He was gone by the time its hoodie-wearing occupants got out and approached his fiancee's home.

CHAPTER THREE

ERIK APPEARED IN the entrance of his rundown Oakland home and a wave of body odor hit Talon's nostrils. His former commanding officer was a disheveled, stinking mess. Long hair clung to his scalp in greasy clumps and a sagging belly pressed against a belt that had run out of notches.

Talon entered the house and struggled to hide his shock. Erik's abode mirrored the sorry state of its broken owner. Fat cockroaches scrabbled among a wasteland of pizza boxes and empty beer bottles.

"Looking good, old friend," Erik slurred.

"The bad guys are keeping me in fighting shape."

Erik grinned at that. "Let me get you a beer."

As Erik headed for his fridge, Talon once again took in the squalor of his surroundings. "Love what you've done with the place."

Erik returned with a bottle of Bud and said, "Fuck you too, man." They toasted and took deep swigs from their beers.

"Man, thanks for coming over. I nodded off and I was back on that fucking mountain..." Erik's voice trailed off. A part of him had never left Afghanistan.

Talon had tried to get through to his former comrade-in-arms on numerous occasions, with little success. His only option left was to be there for Erik during his darkest moments, hoping the man would ultimately find the strength to break free of this terrible downward spiral. For the next two hours, Talon listened to Erik talk about the old days. Good and bad memories competed in his old friend's mind. It was good to reminisce with someone who'd been there.

Eventually, Erik's probing gaze locked on Talon. "So what's going on between you and that reporter broad? Hope you know the girl is crazy about you."

"The feeling is mutual."

"So what are you waiting for? A girl like Michelle comes around once in a lifetime. You don't want to let her get away. Step up to the plate and make an honest woman out of her."

"I just did, a few hours before you called."

"Oh shit, no way. Oh man, I'm so sorry. Fuck, the day you propose you end spending the evening up with a loser like me."

"Don't worry about it."

"I'm proud of you, kid. You two will be great together."

I think so too, Talon thought.

"So what happens next? Might be tougher risking your ass every day knowing there's someone back home waiting for you. A whole family, maybe..."

Talon was impressed by how Erik had redirected the focus from himself. No wonder the man had once earned a reputation as a master interrogator.

"I think it's time for a change." Talon's voice grew dead serious. Erik understood.

"You thinking of leaving the unit?"

"The thought has crossed my mind. I don't want to turn Michelle into just another military wife."

Talon knew this would be the most challenging part of settling down. He loved what he did and took pride in the function his unit served. But he was getting older. Turning his back on the military life would be hard, but he would find a way to serve his country in another capacity. Perhaps he would apply for a job at the CIA or do some teaching.

Despite all his training and lethal skill, Talon harbored no illusions about his mortality. As a soldier at the tip of the spear, the specter of death was his constant companion. Talon had found a way to live with it but he doubted if Michelle could, especially if they decided to start a family.

Erik polished off his beer. "I won't sleep as soundly knowing you're not out there keeping the country safe. But it'll be nice having you around."

Talon hoped that once he settled down in San Francisco, he might become a positive influence on Erik. Would their friendship be enough to conquer the damaged vet's demons? Only time would tell.

Talon finished his beer and checked his watch. It was now past ten. "Alright, I should get going."

Talon walked to the door and paused. "You'll be good, right? You're not going to do anything stupid?"

"If your idea of stupid is ordering a pizza from Joey's and knocking it back with a couple shots of bourbon, then the answer is yes."

The bravado in Erik's voice made Talon want to believe him. "I expect you to be the best man at my wedding."

"Sounds like I don't have long to get my shit together. I think that calls for one more round."

He grinned at Talon and cracked open another beer.

***

Michelle Rossi basked in the happy afterglow of her passionate reunion with Talon and the promise of their shared future. Letting him leave her apartment had not been easy, but she knew his friend needed him. She'd seen Erik a few times since being embedded with the unit and it was clear that the man's psychological scars were far worse than his physical ones. The battlefield could take a heavy toll on the minds and bodies of the brave men and women serving their country.

No one remained unscathed by the experience, not even Talon, but he had found a way to channel every negative thought in a constructive direction and make it work to his advantage. When they first started dating, she wondered what differentiated Talon from other soldiers who succumbed to the stress of their dangerous profession. She'd interviewed many veterans who suffered from post-traumatic stress syndrome and feared Talon could be next in line.

One key element separated Talon from those other warriors. Instead of dwelling on the horrors of combat, he allowed them to fuel the urgency of his mission. Talon never forgot the greater purpose behind the mayhem. Freedom and civilization weren't given to us; they were hard earned over the course of centuries dominated by cruelty and injustice. The battles might be terrible, but the war was worth winning.

Michelle yawned and her eyes grew heavy. It had been a long day. She decided to brew a pot of coffee so she would be awake when Talon returned.

As the stimulating scent of Java beans filled her apartment, her mind turned to the enigmatic man who had so unexpectedly popped back into her life. She was still reeling from the surprising turn her day had taken. When they first met she'd welcomed the idea of a long-distance relationship. She was fiercely independent and didn't want to be beholden to the demands of a full-blown relationship. But each time she saw Talon, it became harder to say goodbye. She was surprised to discover that she wanted him to be part of her life. Not in a let's-see-each-other-when–we-can way, but full-time.

She eyed her engagement ring and stifled a delighted giggle. Her wish was on its way to becoming reality. Did Talon plan to resign from his military duties? The proposal suggested the possibility and the idea of having him around all the time made her grin with happiness.

Her thoughts shifted from Talon to the story she was tackling at the moment. She hadn't offered up any details when Talon asked her about it, but if her source was telling the truth, this piece could rattle Silicon Valley and the entire Bay Area. She needed to proceed with caution.

Michelle was about to take a seat with her laptop when she heard the knock on her door. Could it be Talon? She ruled out that possibility — he had both her car and house keys. Gripped by foreboding, she paused near the door.

"Who is it?"

No answer.

Michelle backed away from the door. She'd found herself in some shady places over the course of her journalistic career and didn't scare easily. Nevertheless, the growing sense that someone threatening lurked behind the door filled her with dread.

Fighting back her fear, she made a go for the couch, where she kept her purse. It contained a can of pepper spray. She was still rummaging in the handbag when a heavy blow rattled the front door. Two more cracks followed in quick succession and after the third sharp crack, the lock snapped.

As the destroyed door swung open, four intruders stood revealed. They all wore baggy black hoodies, their features cloaked in shadow. One carried the kind of battering ram used by police officers.

Michelle's panicked fingers closed around her

pepper spray just as the home invaders swarmed her living room. The intruders wore silver-gray robotic skull-masks under their hoods, and this inhuman presence froze Michelle for a moment. By the time she depressed the nozzle, a gloved hand was already headed for her face. The canister hissed as the intruder's fist connected.

Both Michelle and the pepper spray went flying. Stunned, she tried to regain her bearings. Too late! One of the attackers grabbed her hair.

Many people would have gone rigid with fear at this point, dazed and outnumbered. But Michelle was well versed in martial arts from jujitsu to Krav Maga. Talon had taught her a few tricks, too. Her work took her to some dangerous places and she had to be able to handle herself.

Without hesitation, her elbow fired back and hammered her assailant's collarbone. He let out a cry that was muffled by his robotic mask and backed away.

Michelle spun around and surveyed the living room. Keeping her cool, she searched her environment for everyday objects that could serve as a makeshift weapon. She snatched up the steaming coffee mug from the end table and thrust it into her second attacker's face. The man cursed as the cup exploded in a burst of scalding caffeine and fragmented porcelain.

Suddenly the monstrous quartet before her seemed a little less intimidating. Masks served one function in battle — to instill fear in the enemy. Underneath the armor were flesh-and-blood people who could be hurt. Or killed. Confidence growing, Michelle turned toward her third attacker but this man was prepared. In his gloved hand he held out a Taser.

No!

Compressed nitrogen projected twin probes at 180 feet per second. The projectiles instantly made contact and her body went slack, 50,000 volts overriding her nervous system. As her muscles contracted involuntarily, she hit the floor in a fetal position.

The cold irony was that Michelle now gasped, paralyzed, in the same spot where minutes earlier she'd shared a lover's embrace with Talon.

The intruders gathered around her twitching body, forming a ring of hooded evil. One of the masked men pointed his cellphone camera at Michelle, recording her suffering.

Fucking bastard...

Her will to fight was still there, but her limbs refused to obey her commands. Recognizing her own helpless state, mortal fear set in.

Noooo... Not now. Not like this.

While one masked man recorded Michelle's suffering, the other three produced knives from the pockets of their baggy hoodies. The four figures began to utter foreign words that filled Michelle with atavistic terror.

Oh my God, what's happening here?

At around six-foot-four and the size of a middle linebacker, one man towered over the others. He appeared to be the leader of the group. He sank to his haunches beside Michelle's paralyzed form and produced a canister of spray-paint. There was an explosive hiss as he began to draw an inverted star around her prone form. The paint's nauseating fumes assaulted her nostrils and nearly made her gag.

This can't be happening... Someone, please, help me...

Only one man could stop these monsters, and he wasn't at her side when she needed him the most.

The third assailant placed candles at the points of the floor pentagram and Michelle's dread deepened. The large man leaned over her and whispered in her ear, his voice bereft of all emotion. "I pledge your soul to my master."

With these chilling words, he drove a knife into Michelle's sternum until only the hilt protruded. There had been no hesitation, no dramatic pause, just a robotic precision. Her still-paralyzed body jerked as the blade eased through skin, muscle and bone. The notion that six inches of steel could so easily vanish inside her body seemed surreal, a nightmare beyond her imagining. It couldn't be true... but it was.

To her surprise, she experienced no pain at first. Adrenaline actually masked the damage. Then the big man withdrew his knife and blood streamed from the terrible wound. The first waves of agony washed over her.

Michelle understood that any help would come too late. At the rate she was losing blood, she'd be dead in minutes. In various war zones she'd seen enough people perish, both military and civilians, to know that her fate was sealed.

Talon's face filled her mind as adrenaline surged through her body and her pulse quickened, the increase in blood pressure only hastening her demise.

Her dear Talon. She knew her death would devastate him and for a moment she was more concerned about the man she loved than her own safety.

But the horror was far from over.

It was merely beginning.

Like a school of piranhas descending on live prey, the other knife-wielding monsters plunged their daggers into Michelle with psychotic fury.

In and out, again and again.

Michelle exhaled blood and let out a guttural cry that seemed to intensify her killer's frenzy. The indifferent electronic eyes of their cellphone-cams continued to capture every detail of the bloodbath.

***

Robert Zagan, CEO of Omicron Technologies, entered a sleek, 300-seat auditorium. It was a cavernous chamber appointed in warm woods and brushed steel. Zagan headed for the stage. The company normally used the assembly room to make announcements or even hold press conferences, but today's secret gathering served a far darker agenda.

About eighty seats were filled at the moment. Zagan's audience consisted exclusively of computer engineers, the best and brightest this Silicon Valley tech upstart had produced in the last two years. Their open laptops glowed in the dimly lit chamber like electronic fireflies, the sickly phosphorescent light of their LCD screens bathing their faces in an eerie spectral green. With their hoodies, the programmers seemed like cyber monks tapping away at the secrets of a digital universe. It was an apt analogy, considering what they were working on.

Zagan stepped up to the podium and faced the assembled computer-engineering talent before him. Unlike the coders who favored jeans, Converse and flannel, Zagan was clad in a stylish black suit. His sleek, ascetic features were complemented by a lean, almost gaunt physique — the product of a strict vegan diet and rigid exercise regimen. He'd prematurely gone bald in his mid-twenties and began shaving his head. This only added to his severe presence.

Omicron, like many tech companies that revolutionized the industry and then the world, had come from humble beginnings. Just a few years earlier, the company had consisted of a staff of six. Spurred by rapid growth, Omicron now counted nearly one 500 employees on its 15 acre campus. Its tablets and phones had leveled the playing field and given its competitors a run for their money.

To Zagan's mind, that was just the beginning. The best was yet to come.

Zagan spoke into his mic, uttering esoteric words in the ancient Egyptian liturgical language. The giant screen ignited with quick shots of the hooded figures inside Michelle's apartment. They formed a circle around the helpless woman sprawled on the spray-painted carpet.

The frightening tableau live-streamed in crisp HD through the auditorium on the coders' networked laptop screens. They pounded the keyboards harder.

"I pledge your soul to my master," Zagan proclaimed and the powerfully built killer at Michelle's side repeated the CEO's ominous words. His gleaming blade encompassed the length of the auditorium's mammoth screen, Michelle's terrified features reflected in the broad expanse of steel. When his gloved hand drove the knife into the hapless woman's chest, her scream shredded the silence of the auditorium.

The faces of the employees registered no emotion. Their eyes did glitter with feverish exhilaration as Michelle's final moments flickered on their screens. Fingers flew over the keys, coding in syncopated rhythm with the thrusting blades onscreen as the grisly murder fueled their work. It was as if their workflow kept adjusting to match the speed and intensity of the stabbing knives.

Zagan surveyed his audience with growing satisfaction. He glanced at the big screen, where Michelle's bloodied features loomed. Her eyes were glazing over. As death claimed her, a smile split Zagan's face.

1221111

13332222

Soon the world would experience the terrible power of Omicron.

***

Talon reached Michelle's neighborhood around 11 p.m and found a parking spot right outside her door. Talon's good mood changed the moment he approached the townhome. The door was wide open, its surface splintered. A wave of dread sucked the air from his lungs. Unarmed, he knew he should call the cops first, but Talon wasn't the type to wait around for the cavalry to show up.

He barged into the apartment with quick strides, heart hammering against his ribcage. He was prepared to fight off an army with his bare hands.

When he saw Michelle, an icy hand seemed to tighten around his heart. His mind went blank, his world reduced to the horror before him. The woman he loved was lying in a broken, bloody heap.

Talon had encountered death often enough to know Michelle was gone, but logic took a backseat to emotion. He surged toward the body and cradled her scarlet-streaked head. Blood flowed through his fingers... so much blood... Its coppery tang mixed with her subtle perfume.

He held Michelle in his trembling arms, brushing a sheaf of crimson-caked hair from her face.

God, this can't be happening!

Talon was beyond words and so was the dead

woman in his arms.

He was still cradling Michelle when sirens cut through the night and cops exploded into the apartment, guns pointing at him.

"Step away from the body!"

They were shouting at him, but he didn't hear their words. "I said, step back!"

One of the officers grabbed Talon's arm and something snapped inside of him. Years of training kicked in and he roughly shoved the cop aside. Wrong move. Immediately, three guns were cocked and laser-lights danced over his chest.

Talon slowly raised his hands, his face turning into a dead mask.

CHAPTER FOUR

THE EVENTS FOLLOWING his arrest became a dark blur. Talon remembered the cops slamming him against the wall at gunpoint and slapping cuffs on him. At first he'd refused to back away from Michelle, unwilling to release her body, to let go of her. As long as he clung to her, death wouldn't become permanent and irreversible. His thinking stood in the face of logic but he now found himself in a place where his darkest emotions held reign.

As the police officers kept barking orders at him to back away, his 1000-yard stare fixed on the boys in blue. He was daring them to shoot him, part of him wishing they would put him out of his misery. Another thought prevailed and brought him back to his senses. Michelle was gone but her killer or killers were still out there. This realization tore through his mind and became his reason to go on living. Whoever had done this to his girlfriend would pay for their crimes.

He would make sure of it.

After the cops cuffed Talon, they led him to a waiting cruiser. The red-blue light of the sirens washed over his expressionless features. The long drive to the precinct felt like an endless journey down a dark tunnel, a fragmented, hallucinatory trip into his personal hell. He fixated on his cuffed hands — they were still caked with Michelle's blood — and blocked out the world.

Talon knew he was shutting down. The next thing he remembered was sitting in a bare, gray room facing down two homicide detectives. They were running his prints and soon enough the computer would spit out his service record.

As the detectives launched into their questions, Talon offered up clipped answers. He'd received a call from an old Army buddy. The timing of the texts on his phone would back up his story and they should contact Erik. Not the best alibi in the world, but his old friend would certainly vouch for him.

Two hours into his interrogation they received his service record and the tone in the room started to change. Especially once Detective Jessica Serrone, an attractive Hispanic woman in her late twenties, arrived. At least with her, steely professionalism and hostile suspicion gave way to pity and empathy. He saw that he'd gone from potential murderer to grief-stricken victim, but this only drove home his loss.

The ordeal ended when Detective Serrone told him he was free to go. Before he stepped out of the interrogation room she returned his belongings, including the small box containing Michelle's engagement ring. "I'm sorry for your loss," she said with heartfelt emotion.

Talon turned away from the detective, a man of

stone. He walked into the bustling police precinct and found Erik waiting for him. His old buddy had cleaned up as best he could and the mints almost managed to mask the alcohol on his breath.

Seeing him stirred dark feelings of anger inside Talon. If Erik hadn't been so weak, so needy, none of this would've happened. He would have been with Michelle when the intruders broke into her apartment. He would have kept her safe.

The two soldiers left the precinct without exchanging any words. Erik must've known what was going through Talon's churning mind and remained quiet as they headed for his Mustang.

Rain swept the forlorn streets, a response to the previous day's humidity. Heavy drops pelted the windshield and the wipers were furiously battling the downpour. While Erik navigated the dark, wet roads in uncomfortable silence, Talon's thoughts focused on Michelle. He tried to picture her smiling face but her final, agonizing moments kept intruding on the memory.

"I'm so sorry." Erik's timing on this apology couldn't have been worse. Talon's seething rage bubbled to the surface.

"Stop the car."

"Where are you going to go?" Erik asked.

"None of your goddamn business. Now let me out. I'm not going to ask again."

Erik pulled up to the nearest sidewalk. He was tempted to add something but Talon's glare suggested that he'd better keep his mouth shut.

Talon kicked the door open and disappeared

into the wet night. He walked in the rain until he was soaked. Perhaps he hoped the elements could wash away the darkness inside him and extinguish the fire in his heart.

He tried to recreate in his mind the scene at Michelle's apartment, homing in on details he might have missed at first. One image dominated his thinking — the inverted, five-pointed star scrawled on the floor.

The pentagram.

Did Michelle become the victim of a satanic cult? The notion seemed fantastic, part of a bad B-horror picture from the seventies.

Around six a.m. the first hint of milky sunlight struggled to break through the dense cloud cover and Michelle suddenly seemed to haunt every corner of the city.

When he drifted through Chinatown, it made him think of the hole in the wall restaurant they'd stumbled into one drunken night, only to discover the best dumplings on the planet. Passing Ghirardelli Square, he remembered that Michelle's favorite flavor of chocolate was Dark Cabernet. Who wanted their chocolate to taste like wine? Michelle did.

As he trudged down California Street, he glanced up at the Intercontinental. They had celebrated their first anniversary as a couple in the Top of the Mark rooftop lounge. Overpriced fare, but the view was amazing and Michelle had loved it.

So many memories.

God, he was barely keeping it together.

His long walk led him to Dolores Park. Less than twelve hours earlier he'd proposed to Michelle right in this spot, all thoughts of death far away. He choked back a scream of rage. His hands shook and balled into fists.

Rain fell, as if the city was weeping for the loss of a favorite citizen. The downpour washed away the tears that coursed down Talon's face, but it didn't calm his heaving frame. He couldn't believe that she was gone. That everything they had shared could so easily be lost.

After what seemed like hours, he turned away from the waterfront and continued his silent pilgrimage through San Francisco's rain-soaked urban canyons.

Talon's aimless wanderings drew him back to Michelle's apartment. The structure loomed like a mausoleum, now transformed in Talon's mind into a place of horror. Looking up at the townhome he realized he wasn't ready to set foot in the place again. At least not yet.

He shuffled away from the building and his gaze landed on Michelle's car, still parked on the other side of the street. A parking ticket danced in the wind, held in place by the windshield wiper.

Talon went over to the vehicle and slid behind the wheel. For a brief moment the car offered refuge from the incessant downpour. As soon as he closed the door, he knew he made a mistake. Michelle's scent still lingered here. For a moment he could imagine her sitting beside him again, flashing that beautiful, playful smile.

His eyes fell on the small photograph mounted on the dash. Taken in Afghanistan, it showed him and Michelle grinning like school children. Their smiles were genuine, their happiness palpable.

Looking at the picture pushed him over the edge. Talon knew he needed to numb himself.

Needed to forget.

With a renewed sense of purpose, he headed to the nearest bar and started knocking back shots. The place was a rundown dive and deserted at this mid-afternoon hour. The few lost souls leaning into the well-worn counter were all committed alcoholics and Talon intended to join their ranks.

The whiskey burned as it went down his throat and immediately made him crave another one. Despite his growing buzz, the alcohol wasn't helping Talon forget or calming him down. On the contrary, the booze was adding fuel to the fire. Each shot only stoked the flames inside him.

For the next few days Talon spent his waking hours hitting any watering hole that would take his money. At night he slept off the alcohol at the rundown motel where he'd sought refuge. He didn't shower, didn't eat, didn't give a damn. Terrible thoughts swirled through his mind. His fury was coming to a boil, metastasizing into a murderous rage.

On the third day he ended up in a run-down goth-punk bar. He didn't share anything in common with its patrons except for a hunger to forget.

As the night wore on, he began to notice a crew

of black-clad Goths. The tall, pale leader of the group — a young, cantankerous asshole — would have scored well in a Marilyn Manson lookalike contest. One of the Goth chicks mistook his attention for interest and flashed him a black-lipstick smile. Her wandering eye didn't go over well with her beau. He gave Talon the finger before pulling his girl off the barstool and dragging her toward the exit. His friends filed out after him without paying for their drinks. The bartender hailed expletives after them.

Talon didn't pay attention to the bartender's shouts. All he could think about was the tattoo he'd spotted on the Goth's hand when he flipped him off.

It was an inverted pentagram.

***

Talon followed the brazen gang of Goths for a couple of blocks. A heavy fog shrouded the streets, turning the world into a dreamlike landscape of bleeding shadows.

Talon kept his distance but stayed close enough, never losing sight of his quarry. It soon became apparent where the punks were headed. They were walking toward the Mission Dolores Church and its adjoining cemetery.

The Goths paid little heed to the lone figure trailing them. Even if they spotted him, Talon would offer little cause for alarm. They were four, he was one and in his currently abysmal state, he bore a stronger resemblance to a homeless man than a highly trained killer.

Talon passed through the wrought-iron main gate and began to close the gap once they entered the maze of tombstones.

The fog grew heavier and erased the black-clad punks from view. Focusing on his other senses, Talon tracked the sound of their voices. Their laughter gave way to the hiss of spray canisters. Like a predator drone that had locked on its target, he homed in on the Goths.

The mist cleared and the ring of punks stood revealed. Streaks of graffiti slithered down a vandalized tombstone. The Goths were in the process of painting inverted pentagrams on the headstones. They stopped for a beat, admiring their handiwork, and suddenly became aware of Talon's presence.

For a silent moment the vandals traded glances. Then their leader glared at Talon. "What the fuck you looking at?"

The Goth never finished his sentence as Talon's hand lashed out at him. Now beyond mercy and reason, the Delta Force operator had allowed the alcohol roaring through his system to unleash his killer instinct. His fist connected and sent the raven-haired man crashing into the nearest grave-mound. The crack of bone snapping against the tombstone echoed over the cemetery.

The other Goths stared with big eyes, feet rooted. No one was smiling any longer. Another Goth challenged Talon, fists up. His foolish bravery was rewarded with a vicious series of combination punches that hurled him into a memorial's flowerbed. Before the youth could get up, Talon was upon him, applying a chokehold designed to snap his neck when...

The pitiful cry of one of the Goth chicks pierced Talon's drunken haze of insanity. "Please, don't hurt him, we're sorry..."

Talon stared at the young woman as if waking from a terrible nightmare. Mascara ran down her face in dark streaks. The fear in her eyes was all too real.

Catching his breath, Talon regarded the nearly unconscious kid whose neck he'd almost broken. He studied the punk's pentagram tattoo and realized these weren't hardened killers but a bunch of teenagers playing dress-up.

Talon eyed his hands; they were bloodied from the fight. "Get the hell out of here," he hissed.

The girl blinked at him, almost as if she couldn't quite believe this turn of events. As Talon sank to his knees, the Goths wisely fled the cemetery.

Talon let out a heaving sob and wept. The pouring rain hammered down on his haunted visage, washing away the tears but not the pain.

Not the rage.

The flames of anger burning within him could only be extinguished in one way...

Vengeance.

CHAPTER FIVE

EARLY MORNING SUNLIGHT raked Erik's house. While the incessant downpour had tapered off, Talon's clothes were still wet and streaked with mud and dried blood. Dark rings circled his sunken eyes.

A decision had been made. He wouldn't continue to wallow in self-pity or lash out at the world. Michelle wouldn't want him torn apart by grief. Direct action was required. Her killers still walked the Earth, but their days were numbered. This certainty calmed Talon and filled him with a new sense of purpose.

A new mission.

He knocked on the door, not expecting Erik to show. To his surprise his old friend did emerge. For a moment the two soldiers regarded each other in the gray dawn. For Erik uncertainty mixed with shame.

"I'm sorry about last night," Talon said. He meant what he said. It had been wrong to use Erik as a scapegoat for his own grief and guilt.

Erik's face relaxed. "What are you going to do?"

"What do you think?"

Erik's brows furrowed with concern. "This isn't Afghanistan, Talon. You start going after these fuckers, the cops will hunt you down."

"They can try."

"Let me help you, at least."

"I could use a place to stay, a base of operations."

Erik's eyes flickered at that and the old light edged into them, transforming him into the warrior Talon met on the battlefield all those years ago.

Erik waved him inside. "Mi casa es su casa, compadre."

***

Before Talon could hunt down Michelle's murderers, he needed to get a better feel for his newest enemy. The first order of business was checking the *Chronicle*'s website. Within seconds he found a story on Michelle's murder. The article stated that she'd been stabbed multiple times and also mentioned the fact that her boyfriend discovered the body.

The piece felt like a beat-by-beat replay of the reporting that was dominating local TV news. It touched on the pentagram and theorized about an occult angle, but these salient details didn't seem to elicit much outrage from the public. In a world where terrorists were tweeting decapitation photos of Americans, pentagrams and black candles weren't all that scary anymore. So the world is a madhouse — what else is new?

Talon combed the Internet for other occult crimes committed in the Bay Area over the last few months. His search produced a number of hits. Michelle's murder appeared to be the fifth crime in an escalating series of cases. The one that jumped out the most for Talon was the brutal killing of an Uber driver. Two other murders had occurred at the same time, followed by three suicides. Witness accounts placed some of the suicides near the crime scenes. This prompted speculation about a murder-suicide pact and the possibility that the perpetrators belonged to a cult.

A cult.

This wasn't ISIS, Al Qaeda or one of their many offshoots. This was different. Now he faced a homegrown organization with no discernible political agenda.

What am I up against?

As Talon internalized the articles, he spotted Michelle's byline on a series of them. Finally there was something connecting her to the cult murders. Had her stories turned her into a target?

Talon had seen enough dead reporters to know how dangerous the job could be. Many times he'd wished Michelle did something else for a living. But just as Michelle would never ask him to turn his back on his military career, he couldn't expect her to stop chasing a good story. They were born risk-takers, defined by their willingness to put it all on the line.

Rereading the news items provided little in terms of explanation for why Michelle was singled

WILLIAM MASSA

out by the cult. Her reporting was in-depth and sensitive toward the victims, but it didn't differ substantially from the stories generated by competing news outlets.

Talon decided to head to the paper's offices and talk to Michelle's editor-in-chief, Richard Powell. He might be able to shed some light on the events leading up to her murder.

This time around, stepping into the newspaper offices gutted Talon. Reminders of Michelle were everywhere. Framed awards and articles that bore her name, photographs of her with friends and colleagues whom she'd pointed out to him. He'd entered Michelle's world, and these mementos of her impact on it made her absence even more pronounced.

The receptionist uttered a meek hello and fought back tears. Everyone who saw and recognized him averted their gaze or offered awkward condolences. He appreciated the gesture even though he drew little comfort from their words.

Unnerved by the attention his presence was drawing from the staff, Talon clenched his jaw and picked up his pace. Heading straight into Richard Powell's office, he found the *Chronicle*'s editor-in-chief busy fielding calls.

When Richard noticed Talon, his eyes flashed with surprise. He got off the phone and rushed over, shaking Talon's hand. "I'm so sorry about what happened," Richard said. "Everyone at the paper is in shock. How are you holding up?"

Talon opted not to answer that question. Before

the silence could become uncomfortable, Richard continued. "I spoke with Detective Serrone earlier this morning. She is spearheading the investigation into the cult killings and doing everything in her power to catch these psychos."

For a moment Talon's mind turned back to the Hispanic detective who had offered her condolences to him. "Does the SFPD have any leads?"

"Not to my knowledge, but they're playing it close to the chest on this one, " Richard said.

"I know Michelle did some reporting on these cult crimes. Could that be why this happened?"

"The cops have been asking me the same question, and I'm going to give you the same answer. I don't know. Michelle could be quite secretive when it came to the stories she was working on."

Talon's mood darkened. This wasn't what he'd hoped to hear. "Do you mind if I take a look at her files?"

"I'm afraid that won't be possible. Michelle kept all her work on her laptop. According to the police, her computer and smartphone are missing. I'm sorry I can't be of more help."

Talon nodded and got up. He was almost out the door when Powell addressed him again. "Wait — there's one thing. Michelle believed that the cult had ties to Silicon Valley."

"What do you mean?"

"The three suicides were all tech workers: coders and engineers. It's a competitive industry.

Not every upstart turns into the next Facebook or Apple. For every giant success that makes the news, there are hundreds of failures. The Valley can breed addiction, dysfunction and a sense of entitlement. Maybe even a crackpot cult. It was an angle Michelle was looking into — make of that what you will."

Talon filed this latest detail away for future analysis. He thanked Powell for his time and left the *Chronicle*. His next stop was a local occult bookstore he had Googled earlier.

Talon entered the small shop and shook his head at his macabre surroundings. Esoteric paraphernalia crammed the shelves, ranging from spell kits and ritual supplies to bulk herbs and books on Wicca, Santeria, Norse mythology and every conceivable occult tradition imaginable.

Talon didn't put much stock in any of this superstitious mumbo jumbo. In the battle between science and superstition, science had won a long time ago. It amazed him that so many people still clung to these archaic notions about the world. It was proof that while man was pretty clever, he was still ruled by his hopes and fears.

As he explored the shop, Talon paid little attention to the Tarot cards and Ouija boards. He ignored the vast assortment of crystals and candles. Instead, he bee-lined straight for the section dealing with satanic rituals.

Talon felt uncomfortable in the otherworldly store; it seemed to have been designed to eschew all forms of natural light. The owners were selling the idea of a transcendent experience. Combined with the New Age soundtrack being piped through the loudspeaker system, the décor achieved the desired effect.

Talon wasn't a superstitious man but ten years of war with fanatics in the Middle East had taught him both the power and the danger of misguided faith in the supernatural. It could turn murder into a holy act and justify the most terrible of crimes, crimes committed in the name of God. Even though he didn't believe in the Devil, Talon did believe in knowing your enemy. If Michelle's killer worshipped the Prince of Lies, Talon wanted to understand what drove him (or her) to such monstrous acts.

As Talon eyed the shelves of books classified under Satanism, he groaned inwardly at some of the titles. Massive doorstops like *THE HISTORY OF THE DEVIL* and *SERVING DARKNESS* promised something a little different than light beach reading.

A waif-like store clerk sidled up to him. Her myriad tattoos and alabaster skin conjured the illusion that she was attuned to some other frequency than the rest of humanity.

She flashed Talon her most mysterious smile. "You look like you may need some help."

"Is it that obvious?"

"Let's just say you don't seem like the type who shops here."

"And what type is that?"

The clerk's lips curled into another one of her knowing smiles, but she didn't offer an explanation.

Talon forged ahead. "I need a few general books on the occult. The basics."

The young woman nodded and fished out a series of seminal texts. Talon barely scanned the titles – he was way out of his comfort zone here.

"It's difficult to narrow down to the basics in a field as diverse as the supernatural, but these should make for a good start."

Inspecting the books, Talon decided that this would do for now. He paid for his purchases, left the store and headed back to Erik's house.

There, he opened the main gate and walked past Erik's home, heading for a small guesthouse separated by a minuscule yard. Erik had been cool enough to let Talon crash in his father's old office, which had stood empty since the heart attack that led to his passing. The studio contained a small bed, a worn desk and years worth of dust. It would do fine. Talon had stayed in far worse places.

As he took a seat on the squeaking bed and fired up his laptop, a plan was forming in the back of his mind.

Learn about the enemy.
Identify the enemy.
Exterminate the enemy.

He had two more weeks before he needed to report back to duty. Two weeks to win this war. He wouldn't leave San Francisco without completing his mission.

Talon checked his email. There was a ton of spam and a message from a general who had received word of the tragedy. Most of his Delta buddies hadn't contacted him, and in a way he was glad. In time the news would get around and the condolences would begin to flood his inbox.

For now he would rather not become distracted by reminders of his military life. The new mission would demand his complete focus and attention.

Talon removed the newly acquired books from his backpack and began to familiarize himself with the material. After two hours of reading about cults and satanic rituals, the letters became a blur and he could no longer concentrate on the dense, morbid texts. He wanted to understand what he was up against, but he was foremost a man of action. Talon was itching to be out in the field. Rage swirled inside him and his mind kept wandering back to Michelle.

His beautiful Michelle, now gone forever.

Hands shaking, Talon slammed the book shut and closed his eyes.

Goddammit, pull yourself together!

The mental command seemed hollow and lacked conviction. The walls of Erik's cramped guesthouse felt like they were closing in on him and he couldn't shake a growing feeling of claustrophobia. He had to get out of here.

Time to engage in a different form of intelligence gathering. He was going to revisit the scene of the crime. Perhaps there was some telltale sign the cops had missed when they combed Michelle's apartment. Some clue that could point him in the right direction. Something. Talon knew he was grasping at straws here, but he was a desperate man. Desperate, but also determined.

His eyes fell on a nearby dresser. Two items rested on its surface – a Glock 41 Gen4 in a shoulder holster, and a Ka-Bar in a tactical sheath. Presents from Erik. "My gut tells me these might come in handy," Erik had said with a low chuckle. Talon had a feeling they might.

He snatched up the pistol and knife, then stepped out of the guesthouse. A beaten-up motorcycle was gathering dust in the driveway. Erik hadn't ridden his Ducati in over a year but encouraged Talon to use the bike to get around town. Talon extricated the keys.

The long-dormant engine squelched and gurgled before screaming back to life. He thought he could hear a couple of neighbors slamming their windows shut but Talon welcomed the noise. The ferocious roar drowned out his dark thoughts as he powered down the street. There was only the road, the fierce sound of the Ducati and the fire in his soul. For a brief moment, Talon could pretend that the wailing engine sounds were the screams of Michelle's murderers.

Forty-five minutes later he pulled up to Michelle's townhome and was gripped with dread. Part of him wished he didn't have to set foot in the apartment where he'd discovered Michelle's ruined body. The feeling of helplessness he associated with the place returned with a vengeance.

Talon gave himself an internal push and approached the front door. Police lines served as a grim reminder of Michelle's murder but now dangled forlornly from one side of the doorframe instead of barricading the entrance.

Has someone entered the crime scene?

Talon's hand closed around the door-handle and froze.

Muffled footsteps and voices could be heard behind the door. Someone was definitely inside Michelle's unit.

Talon's fingers touched the Glock sitting in his armpit sling. Reassured by the weight of the gun, he turned the knob in a slow, deliberate manner. The lock wouldn't snap open to announce his arrival. Instead the door parted soundlessly, opening a few inches.

Three men were busy combing the place. They remained oblivious to his presence, focused on the task at hand. All three of them wore expensive looking suits. Talon thought it doubtful that these guys were Feds or homicide detectives. Call it gut instinct, but they were way too sleek and polished to be law enforcement.

The two bigger men moved with precision and grace despite their size. Talon pegged them as retired military. The youthful guy carried himself with authority. He had to be the one in charge.

"What are you people doing here?" Talon demanded. He took a step toward the leader of the group and one of the big men reached for him.

Big mistake.

Talon wrenched the guy's arm and using the big man as a human battering ram, he shoved him into his incoming partner. The two bodyguards hunched over into balls of pain.

One of the downed guards went for the bulge under his jacket but a quick hand signal from the boss stopped him.

Talon regarded the man they were protecting. The leader stood his ground without flinching, eyes betraying no fear. "I know you're angry and want to lash out at someone, Sergeant Talon, but putting my assistants in the hospital won't bring Michelle back."

How does this guy know my name?

"I apologize for my men's overeager dedication to their profession, but we're not your enemy."

"Could've fooled me." Talon took a step closer, eyes blazing. "Who the hell are you?"

A thin smile played over the leader's face and his voice became flat and determined. "My name is Simon Casca and I'm the man who's going to help you hunt down the monsters who murdered your girlfriend and kill every single one of them."

CHAPTER SIX

TALON AND SIMON Casca now fronted the small balcony of Michelle's apartment. A ravenous fog had swallowed the city and the moist air prickled Talon's face. Below, cars zipped down the street, the mist transforming them into ghostly shapes. Muted sounds of traffic drifted through the thick layers of condensation.

If Casca was to be believed, Talon now shared the balcony with one of the richest men in California, if not the entire U.S. He was the owner of Xtel, a company that manufactured twenty-five percent of all microchips currently in use. Xtel wasn't a sexy stock on the rise, but the company had been around since the dawn of the Silicon Age.

Talon studied Casca. The billionaire looked young, boyish almost, and appeared to be in his mid-twenties. Unlike most of his Silicon Valley compatriots, he favored slim, well-turned-out Prada suits. "I'm still waiting for you to tell me what you're doing here," Talon said.

"I'm here for the same reason you are. I'm looking for answers."

Talon processed these words. Casca's security

team was visible behind the balcony's sliding doors. Still massaging their bruised bodies and egos, the two men stole nervous glances at him.

Casca followed Talon's gaze. "They're both former Marines and don't spook easily. Your reputation is well deserved."

"What reputation? You don't know anything about me."

"I know *exactly* everything about you, Sergeant Mark Talon. You're one of the most decorated soldiers in the entire Armed Forces. Two tours with the 101st Airborne Division, followed by your current assignment with Delta Force."

"On paper my unit doesn't even exist, so how did you get this information?"

"There are no more secrets once you're worth north of a billion dollars."

"So you've been throwing some of that funny money around. Question is, why?"

"When a friend is murdered I like to know who the players are."

This revelation caught Talon off guard. "You knew Michelle?"

Casca nodded. "Michelle interviewed me a couple years back and we stayed in touch. Three weeks earlier she contacted me, asking for help. She needed to draw on my field of expertise."

"And what field would that be?"

"Fringe religions. Ancient rituals. Demonology. The occult." He paused, letting the words sink in. "How much do you know about the paranormal, Sergeant?"

"I'm a little too old to believe in ghosts and goblins."

"I guess that answers my question."

"There's evil out there, but it wears a human face. Michelle's killers may think the Devil is real, but they're just flesh and blood." Talon took a step closer. "What sort of cult are we dealing with here?"

"Michelle asked me the same question. We don't have much to work with at the moment, but certain details suggest a computer-technology cult of some kind. These types of cults incorporate science fiction and computer concepts into their occult and magical doctrine. You may be familiar with the "Rama" cult, whose members committed mass suicide and believed their spiritual guru to be in communication with aliens. Or Aum Shinrikyo, which carried out a Sarin gas attack on the Tokyo subway in 1995."

Talon nodded grimly. "Aum Shinrikyo – Supreme Truth – was designated a terrorist organization by the United States. The cult used Christian and Buddhist ideas as well as the writings of Nostradamus to attract a highly educated following. Their leader, Asahara, saw himself as a Christ-like figure destined to save his followers from nuclear Armageddon."

"I'm impressed, Sergeant. You know your terrorist groups."

"What makes you think we're dealing with such a group?"

"Besides the three suicides and their ties to

Silicon Valley, there's a telling detail the cops have been keeping a lid on."

Casca indicated for Talon to follow him back into the apartment. As they returned to the crime scene, Talon tried to avoid the discoloration on the floor, knowing all too well its origin.

Casca respectfully circled the chalk outline of Michelle's body and for a moment, a second pentagram on the wall framed his head like an unholy halo. He tilted his head at the series of numbers – a combination of ones and zeroes – scrawled below the inverted star:

1010011010

Talon had missed the numbers when he last set foot in Michelle's place. Seeing a loved one crumpled in a puddle of gore could impact anyone's situational awareness.

"It's a binary number," Talon said.

"Correct. As you may know, binary numbers can be converted both into letters and decimal numbers. The number you're looking at translates to six-six-six."

666. The number of the Beast.

"According to Michelle's source in the SFPD, the three suicides had the same binary number tattooed on their forearms."

Talon took a step closer. The dark color of the numbers suggested that they were etched in blood.

Michelle's blood.

"There's something else you need to be aware of... I apologize in advance for bringing up such a painful and gruesome subject. The forensic report revealed that Michelle was stabbed eighteen times with three different knives. Six thrusts for each blade. Based on the angle of the wounds, the police think there were at least three killers involved, each wielding a blade."

Talon balled his fists, his nails digging into the palms of his hands. How could Casca have access to secret police information? The answer was simple. Money. Information came at a price and Casca possessed deep pockets. And that begged another question. Why was he willing to part with his cash and get involved in an occult murder case? What was his angle?

"How does the head of a billion-dollar tech company end up becoming an expert on the weird?" Talon said.

"Even billionaires need hobbies." Casca managed a thin smile before his features grew serious again. "I inherited Xtel. The company's achievements are the result of my father's hard work and vision. I'm the CEO in name only. Meaning that I attend a few board meetings but leave the day-to-day operations to folks far more qualified than myself. My calling lies in a different area."

There was a part of Casca's story that didn't quite add up in Talon's mind. Rich guys didn't spend their free time chasing shadows and studying apocalyptic cults. "Do you believe the cult targeted Michelle?"

"I don't believe in coincidence."

"That makes two of us. But why her? Every major news outlet has been running stories about these occult crimes."

"I don't think Michelle was killed because of an article she wrote. She was killed because of an article she was going to write."

"What do you mean?"

"Michelle had a source connected to the cult. They must've found out she was talking with someone on the inside, and they retaliated."

Casca's latest revelation confirmed Talon's worst suspicion. He trembled with emotion.

My girl died because of a story she was working on.

Michelle's high-risk job had cost her her life. But death didn't catch up with her in some far-flung, war-ravaged or disease-ridden Third World country. It found her here in San Francisco, in her own home.

Casca leaned closer, his voice growing determined. "We find Michelle's source, we find her killers."

CHAPTER SEVEN

"WE FIND MICHELLE'S source, we find her killers."

Good plan but where to start? As Talon mentally ran through his options, he remembered the Skype conversation he'd interrupted when he first arrived at the *Chronicle*. What had Michelle said again?

"Just one of my sources."

Could that woman be the source Casca was talking about? Talon recalled her nervous expression. At the time, he'd dismissed it as just run-of-the-mill camera shyness – not everyone felt comfortable in front of a webcam – but now he wasn't so sure. It was a long shot, but worth looking into.

He rang the *Chronicle* and asked Powell to run a quick check of Michelle's Skype calls. She'd used her desktop during the Skype call, so it should be easy to track her conversations. A few minutes later, Powell offered up a name – Becky Oakes – and a phone number.

Talon considered his next move. Calling Becky might spook her. If indeed Becky turned out to be the leak, he'd have to tread with caution. In all likelihood the cult had gone after her too. There hadn't been any reports of other murders, though. Maybe she'd gotten lucky and escaped.

Casca had urged Talon to contact him if he needed anything. Talon wasn't keen on further involving the billionaire, but he did have the pull to gain access to classified information.

Talon texted Becky's info to Casca. Less than an hour later, Talon received an email containing the results of a detailed background check.

Twenty-three years old, Becky was an attractive brunette with big, intelligent eyes and perfect skin. Computer-science major. She'd been an assistant at Omicron, one of Silicon Valley's biggest tech companies, for the last eight months.

Talon skimmed the rest of the detailed report. There were credit card histories, outstanding student loans and even notes regarding Becky's recent emails and phone calls.

For a surreal moment, Talon could almost pretend he was conducting some military operation instead of embarking on a vigilante mission of vengeance.

Analyzing the report further, Talon learned that Becky lived in the Mission District. As an assistant, she wouldn't be raking in the big bucks. So how was she able to afford the $3000-a-month rent of a one-bedroom apartment in that area?

The next paragraph of the report provided an explanation. Becky had been dating George Soldes, a computer engineer at Omicron and one of the suspected cult members who jumped off the

Golden Gate Bridge. Had the suicide motivated Becky to seek out the press, dooming Michelle in the process?

Only Becky could answer that question.

Talon mounted Erik's motorcycle and tore off toward the Mission District. Zipping through the hilly streets, his thoughts turned to the enigmatic new figure who had entered the picture. Who was Simon Casca? Talon still wasn't quite sure what to make of the youthful billionaire. He was intense yet projected sincerity and a nearly fanatical passion about his esoteric field of expertise.

Casca seemed determined to help. Still, without fully understanding whatever motivation was driving his newfound benefactor, Talon would keep his guard up. He planned to delve deeper into Casca's background later but at the moment his first priority was tracking down Becky Oakes.

Traffic was light during the mid-afternoon hours and it didn't take long for Talon to arrive at Becky's apartment complex. He waited in front of the main entrance. As soon as the first person stepped out of the building, he used the opportunity to slip through the open door. If Becky was around, he hoped to catch her off guard and not give her a chance to cook up some cover story.

Becky lived on the third floor and Talon easily located her apartment. He determined that the door was unlocked – it didn't bode well. Glock leading the way, he walked into the unit.

Broken furniture, overturned shelves and piles of computer books lay scattered on the floor. There was no sign of Becky. Did she escape in time, or was she now in the cult's clutches?

His cellphone vibrated and Casca's voice grew audible on his headset. "What's the situation?"

"Looks like we're running a few steps behind. They broke into her place and tore it apart. Girl's not here."

"This cult isn't big on hiding the bodies. She could be laying low somewhere."

"My feelings exactly."

Talon studied the apartment, his eyes roaming. Who was Becky Oakes? Who were her friends? What would be her options, given what they knew about her?

"Any theories as to where she might be holed up?"

"My assistant is going through Ms. Oakes' phone records as we speak."

Once again Talon didn't know if he should be impressed or worried about Casca's ability to attain private information.

"Besides her boyfriend and parents, the one phone number that keeps coming up belongs to Janice Goldstein. They both interned at Google a few months ago. Judging from her social network activity, they're best friends. Last call between them was two days ago."

The day Michelle was murdered, Talon thought. If there had been any doubt about Becky's involvement, this seemed to erase it. It was all beginning to make sense in his mind. In the wake of Michelle's murder Becky had gone off the grid, ditching her phone and avoiding all social networks. That was wise — the people after her were computer wizards and could track her digital footprints.

Janice Goldstein was Talon's best lead. With any luck she could lead him to Becky.

An hour later, he was staking out Janice's workplace, some new app developer called *Snapshut* with offices on Freemont Street. Like Becky, Janice had recently graduated from intern to assistant. Most likely, she'd be working crazy hours. Talon knew he'd better brace himself for a long night.

He found a coffee shop facing the *Snapshut* offices and sipped on a cup of bitter black brew that set him back four bucks. The price made him cringe – what was happening to this country?

Keeping track of the steady flow of people on the sidewalks had a soothing, almost hypnotic effect on Talon. His new detail couldn't have been more different from the arid monotony of Afghanistan.

As he kept watch, a Google bus pulled up to the curb and dropped off a boatload of Silicon Valley workers. They carried themselves in a casual and carefree manner, dressed like eternal teenagers with fat allowances. Distressed jeans, expensive sneakers and grungy t-shirts that all came with designer labels easily spotted by the knowing eye. Every one of them sported backpacks containing tablets or laptops.

Talon figured they'd been putting in some quality time in front of their computers during their air-conditioned commute. He'd read about the private shuttles that scooped up workers from their San Francisco neighborhoods and brought them to their Silicon Valley tech enclaves. Late at night the buses would return and so would the workers.

The tech elite had become shadows who barely participated in their local communities. The big companies provided food, haircuts, dental appointments, gym equipment, laundry, dry cleaning – there was no need to shop or interact locally. In many ways, companies like Omicron had already become cults that indoctrinated their disciples with an ideology designed to separate them both physically and psychologically from the rest of the world. Technology was their God and material success their salvation.

Janice suddenly emerged from her workplace. She headed straight for the coffee shop – just another part of her daily routine. A quick pick-me-up at the end of a long day. Phone cradled under her ear, she approached the barista.

Talon stealthily pointed his cell at her. He pulled up an app Casca had told him to download earlier and scanned the shop for Bluetooth signals. He selected Janice's phone from the list and pressed "Force-Pair." Once that was done, he pushed a button labeled "Install.Exe." A bar filled the screen as his phone hacked into Janice's.

By the time Janice grabbed her drink and left the café, the installation of the hacking program was complete. Talon followed while he listened in on Janice's conversation. Her voice sounded concerned. Talon felt like a creep for spying on the woman's private exchange.

When Janice addressed the other party on the line as Becky, however, Talon's eyes widened with triumph. Judging from the phone number on his spy app, Becky wasn't using her old cell. She had probably purchased a disposable phone with a prepaid SIM card. *Smart girl.* It sounded like she wanted to meet up with Janice at nearby Yerba Buena Garden.

Talon rushed toward his motorcycle. He would beat Janice to the rendezvous point.

Darkness encroached Yerba Buena Garden as his bike sidled up to the curb. The park covered two blocks with well-tended gardens and provided a much-needed escape from the hustle and bustle of San Francisco.

Talon combed the park and within minutes located Becky near the Dr. Martin Luther King Jr. Memorial Fountain. Spotlights inside the waterfall cast Becky in stark silhouette. Water gurgled as she paced up and down the shining slabs of glass inscribed with excerpts from Dr. King's speeches.

Becky's paranoid gaze swept the surrounding area and lingered on Talon. He sped up his approach and Becky turned on her heel, heading off in the opposite direction.

Shit! She'd made him.

As Becky surged up a nearby flight of stairs that led away from the fountain, Talon cranked up his pace. Had his over-eagerness betrayed him? Or was he not used to stalking targets within an American city?

Talon reached the top of the stairs and spotted Becky as she shot down a walkway.

She was crossing the next street when a black van zoomed toward her. Tires screeched as the van ground to a halt and the door was flung open. Two men decked out in black hoodies jumped out of the vehicle and snatched a shocked Becky. She immediately went limp in the kidnappers' arms and Talon realized that they must've Tasered her. Bastards! The hooded abductors whisked Becky's convulsing form into the van.

Talon considered his options. He could pull his gun and prevent them from getting away, but his rescue attempt was liable to backfire. There were too many witnesses, not to mention the possibility of the cops showing up before he could question Becky's attackers.

Talon opted to follow the van instead. He'd deal with them in a more private setting. Nevertheless, he experienced a twinge of anxiety as the doors slammed shut and the vehicle burned rubber. If he lost them and something happened to Becky, her death would be on his conscience.

Talon rushed back to his motorcycle, eyes trailing the black van as it rounded the park. Seconds later, he eased into traffic and picked up the chase. He kept a safe distance but never lost sight of the vehicle in front of him. Talon prayed that Becky's captors wouldn't harm her in transit.

Hopefully he'd made the right call. A vision of dead Michelle popped into his mind, and this only sharpened his focus. He wouldn't let these freaks get away with murder a second time.

He trailed the van for half an hour until it finally pulled up to a sleek, expensive-looking house. It was one of the growing numbers of eco-homes that were in vogue in the Bay Area: oblong windows, high-quality wood, solar panels and plants on the roof. The low-impact materials were designed to reduce the home's carbon footprint.

Whoever lived here wasn't hurting financially, that was for sure.

The van rolled up the driveway and into the garage. Talon slowed down. His lips twisted into a merciless smile and his soul turned to ice. He was looking forward to getting better acquainted with Becky's abductors.

CHAPTER EIGHT

BECKY OAKES EYED her kidnappers inside the moving van and knew she was staring at her future murderers. Her body ached and throbbed and she could barely move, muscles useless in the wake of the vicious Taser attack. When her abductors first snatched her, Becky had recognized one of them. His name was Jeff and he was a star engineer at Omicron. She suspected that the other men were her fellow co-workers, too. What had happened to these programmers to make them turn into cold-blooded killers?

She'd been asking herself that question since the moment she first walked into Omicron's assembly hall and witnessed a murder unspooling on the HD jumbo screen. Her boyfriend George was one of the coders in the auditorium, busily programming away as Zagan dominated the horror show onstage. Seeing he beau as an indifferent witness to the slaughter shattered her world and wounded her to the core.

To be fair, their relationship had been falling apart for some time now. George had become cold and they stopped making love. At first she assumed he might be dating someone else and the distancing was his passive-aggressive way of working up to an official break-up. But it soon became clear that something far more disturbing was unfolding here.

One clue was the strange binary tattoo on George's forearm; a tattoo she noticed on a growing number of tech workers at Omicron. Becky confronted George about the tattoo, but this only pushed him away. He stopped calling her and soon she only saw him at work, when it couldn't be avoided.

Their relationship was over. So what possessed her to follow her ex into the main auditorium that fateful night, when she was working late? The presence of guards near the doors of the assembly hall made her frown. Fortunately, she knew of a back way that led to the auditorium's balcony.

Giving in to curiosity, she made a go for the less-guarded second entrance.

This turned out to be the biggest mistake of her life.

After witnessing that monstrous scene inside the auditorium, she found herself at a loss. What should she do? Who could she reach out to for help? She feared that if she went to the cops they would laugh at her and word would soon get back to Omicron. Who knew what might happen if her colleagues realized she had witnessed their crime. Nothing good, that was for certain.

A day later George committed suicide and obviously this news rattled her further. The man she'd started dating three months ago was full of life and hope for the future. Like many of the young computer talents in start-up land, George was driven and empowered by a sense of manifest destiny. He was going to play his role in shaping the technologies of the world to come. The George she knew was a far cry from the man who took a dive off the Golden Gate Bridge.

Becky's first sign of hope came when Michelle rang her and wanted to talk about George's suicide. It didn't take much convincing for her to break down and spill her story. But somehow the cult found out about the meeting. And now they'd found her.

The van stopped and the door was opened. Rough hands reached for her and she felt herself being dragged out of the parked van and into a garage. She fought back weakly but her muscles were still recovering from being zapped by the Taser. Once inside the living area, one of the kidnappers switched on the recessed lights, revealing a tastefully decorated home. Incongruously, a plastic tarp had been laid out over the hardwood floor in anticipation of Becky's arrival.

The three hooded men hefted Becky's limp body onto the plastic and her eyes grew wet with terror. She held no illusions about what was going to happen next. The news stories about Michelle's grisly murder popped into her mind. All she could do now was pray that the end would be swift and relatively painless.

The ring of urban monks slipped on their robotic

skull-masks and whipped out their knives.

"Please you don't have to do this-"

One of the cultists taped her mouth shut with duct tape, silencing her.

Oh God, let it be over soon...

The blades drew closer. Becky closed her eyes.

And that's when the van's alarm shattered the silence of the sleepy nighttime neighborhood outside.

***

The glass-paneled front door swung open and one of the hooded kidnappers emerged from the eco-house. Without the intimidating robot mask, his harmless countenance stood in sharp contrast to the brutal act he'd been ready to commit moments earlier. He stalked up to the SUV and killed the alarm.

Talon lurked in the thick bushes that lined the driveway. Features hidden by a black balaclava, hands covered in leather gloves, silencer mated with his Glock. The moment the cult member turned his back on him, he darted into the open home.

Outside, the cultist finished his inspection. Reassured that no car thief was hanging around the property, he headed back into the house. As soon as he closed the door, Talon's gloved hand reached for his throat from the dead corner of the door. He wrenched the man's neck back with a bone-snapping crack and caught the lifeless body before it could slump to the ground.

Without making a sound, Talon lowered the cultist to the floor and edged deeper into the house.

The other cultists never turned around as Talon stepped into the living room. Their attention was entirely devoted to the upcoming blood sacrifice.

Talon met Becky's terrified gaze.

The two men must have read the change in their victim's expression, because they finally spun around. Talon never blinked as he fed the first cult member two bullets.

The robotic mask erupted in a hail of fiberglass, blood and brain matter, the bullet punching out a fist-sized exit wound.

The cultists hit the tarp and painted it red. Only muffled sounds emanated from beneath the duct tape covering Becky's mouth.

The third cultist faced Talon, blade up, aware that he stood no chance against the Glock aimed at him.

"Drop the knife and you'll live," Talon said.

He was lying.

They'd forfeited their lives when they murdered Michelle. Talon was merely hoping to interrogate the last man before permitting him to join his two buddies in hell.

Talon was a soldier, not a vigilante. He'd killed his share of terrorists and enemy combatants but didn't go around taking out civilians, much less Americans. But he felt zero regret about showing these two bastards the high cost of war.

The cultist straightened and uttered a few words in a language Talon didn't comprehend. Whoever was hiding behind that freaky mask was smart enough to know that you didn't bring a knife to a gunfight. Nevertheless, what he did next caught Talon off guard. Without hesitation, the man drove his own blade through the bottom of his jaw, straight into the base of his brain. He collapsed in a writhing mass of gushing red.

Talon could've put him out of his twitching misery with a quick bullet to the heart, but the Delta Operator was fresh out of mercy. Talon watched in silence as the man drowned in his own blood.

CHAPTER NINE

BECKY FACED TALON and her haunted eyes blinked back tears. The woman was in shock, shutting down. Who could blame her? Minutes earlier she'd stared down certain death. Now she sat at the oak dining-room table in the adjoining kitchen, eyes fixed on nothing.

Talon wished he could offer her some coffee or a drink to settle her nerves, but the risk of leaving circumstantial evidence behind was too high. Better if they got out of here as soon as possible. Talon doubted that the neighbors had heard anything that would make them call the cops, but why press his luck?

Appraising Becky's condition, he concluded that she was in no state for a ride on his motorcycle. Talon called Casca and the billionaire picked up on the second ring.

"How did it go?" he asked.

"Becky is safe and the cult is three members short."

"Didn't want to spare at least one for questioning?"

"I tried, but he wouldn't play ball."

"Where are you?"

"Still at the house. I could use a pickup."

"I'm sending a car from my downtown office. Expect them to arrive within minutes."

Casca clicked off. Talon's gaze shifted to the quivering woman. He removed his balaclava. The poor girl needed to see a human face, not another masked assassin. Becky didn't strike him as the type that would repay her rescuer by picking him out of a police lineup.

"Who are you?" she asked.

Talon considered how to answer. He could be the one asking the questions and risk Becky retreating into her own bubble. Or he could tell the truth and hopefully earn her cooperation. Talon opted for the second approach.

"Mark. I'm Michelle's boyfriend."

It took a moment for the words to register. A tear trickled down Becky's cheek as the pieces clicked together in her mind. "I'm so sorry. It's all my fault. If I hadn't contacted her..."

She broke off.

"Tell me what you know," Talon said.

Becky complied. In a halting voice that gained confidence as Becky went deeper into her terrible ordeal, she recounted what she'd witnessed at Omicron. When she reached the part where she contacted Michele, Talon interrupted. "How'd the cult find out you were talking to the press?"

"I'm not sure. After I told Michelle what I experienced, she asked me to get some tangible evidence. Without proof she wouldn't dare run my story. I needed to bring her something that we could take to the cops. I never got a chance."

She didn't have to say any more.

Omicron's security cams had probably spotted Becky sneaking into the meeting. It wouldn't take much for them to hack her computer and discover that she'd been in contact with the *San Francisco Chronicle*.

"After I spoke with Michelle, I was too scared to go home. I spent the night with my best friend Janice. I only heard about what happened to Michelle the next day. That's when I knew they were looking for me."

"Where did you go after that?"

"I found a motel. I didn't want to endanger Janice. For two days I tried to figure out what my next move should be. I was about to take my chances and go to the cops when..." Becky paused, overwhelmed by the memory of her brush with death. Talon guessed that along the way she'd probably made a mistake and left some sort of digital footprint. Or Omicron had hacked her phone records and found out about Janice Goldstein the same way Casca had.

Talon's cell chirped and he scanned the incoming message. Becky's ride had arrived and the driver was circling the block. "Becky, a car is about to take you someplace safe."

Panic invaded her face and Talon knew she needed a reassurance stronger than words. He gently touched her arm. Leaning closer, he said, "You have to trust me, Becky. My friend will make sure nothing happens to you. Do you understand what I'm saying?"

Becky nodded.

Talon led her outside of the house. She was traumatized but kept her composure.

He scoped the neighborhood for any potential witnesses but the sidewalks remained deserted. Headlights speared the night and a black BMW pulled up to the curb.

A tinted window rolled down, revealing the face of one of Casca's security men. The big man managed a reassuring smile as Talon assisted Becky into the luxury car.

"You'll be safe, Becky." Talon caught a whiff of fine leather as he closed the car door behind her. The BMW edged into the road.

Talon strode back into the house and paused before the seeping bodies. The cultist's high-quality Halloween masks appeared to be from *The Terminator,* or at least inspired by the iconic film's design. The living room resembled the grim battlefield in a post-apocalyptic science-fiction flick.

Talon stripped off the masks. Like his first kill, these two cultists looked like harmless computer geeks. All three men sported the 666 binary tattoos. Talon wondered what initiation rite had earned the cultists their mark of the Devil, and feared the answer.

Checking their belongings, he came across Omicron worker-identification badges. The evidence was rapidly mounting against the tech company.

Turning away from the bodies, Talon searched the home. Except for the three dead cultists, the elegant dwelling offered few hints as to the dark predilections of its inhabitants. Talon did spot a few occult books and a set of black candles on a library shelf. A deck of Tarot cards sat near the paranormal paraphernalia. Three cards poked from the deck: The Devil, the Hanged Man and the Death card.

The spooky, medieval images triggered renewed confusion in Talon. Had a creepy hobby metastasized into a twisted philosophy that encouraged human sacrifice? How exactly had occult rituals mated with 21st Century computer technology? Something had turned these computer-geeks into fanatics who were willing to die for their misguided beliefs.

And kill for them.

Once Talon completed his search of the house, he scooped up the dead cultists' cell phones. He also grabbed a laptop that sat on the oak table, its screen splattered with blood.

He knew Casca would want to study the computer's data. The billionaire had come through for him twice now. Though he hated to admit it, he was glad to have someone with Casca's means and level of influence on his side. Talon was used to working within a unit and knew that firepower and skill weren't always enough. Intel, resources and the proper backup could be crucial in shaping the final outcome of any conflict.

Talon filled up a black satchel with evidence

and wiped off all the surfaces Becky might have come in contact with. Inspiration struck him as he studied the password-protected Omicron cell phone. He keyed in the cult's trademark binary number and the home-screen popped up, its data at his full disposal. There were text messages and emails to go through, but for now he was more interested in the photos and videos on the phone.

Becky's shocking experience in the Omicron auditorium popped into his mind. If she was telling the truth these cultists not only killed and filmed their murders but also streamed them to their unholy flock.

Had they recorded Michelle's murder? The thought filled Talon with a mixture of horror and rage. Like a man possessed he went through the cultist's videos. He located the first recording and pressed play. The footage showed Becky weakly fighting back inside the van.

Talon continued his search. After three more unrelated videos, he found the one he dreaded to view. His pulse quickened as Michelle's final moments unspooled before him. The sound of her fear-stricken voice in the eco-home felt like a distant whisper from beyond the grave. As the merciless masked killers closed in on their downed victim, Talon's fingers whitened around the body of the phone and nearly snapped its case.

Twenty seconds into it, before the knife had reached her, he stopped the video. He didn't want to relive the murder. Couldn't. Inhaling sharply, he turned off the phone. The screen went black and so did Talon's mind. Rational thought was swept aside by a white-hot rage.

He was going to bring down the whole damn cult.

The vibrating cell in his hand pulled him out of his dark thoughts. It was an incoming text message from an unknown number. The ominous text read: *We're ready to begin.* A second later, the cultist's phone chirped and the Skype logo flashed on the screen.

The perverted monsters on the other end of the line were eager to bear witness to the latest sacrifice. For a moment, Talon hesitated. What should he do? His eyes fell on the dead cultists.

If they wanted a bloody show, they'd get one.

A show they wouldn't soon forget.

***

The jumbo-sized screen inside Omicron's auditorium came alive with a HD view of the eco-house. Zagan wore his trademark suit and robot skull-mask, projecting the image of a high priest from some dark future. Shifting his attention to the incoming image, Zagan immediately recognized that something was wrong. Someone had flipped the script on him.

Onscreen, a camera panned through the living room and captured a disturbing set of images. Instead of a hapless victim, the lifeless features of Zagan's followers jumped into view, the bodies neatly lined up side by side. Dead eyes peered back at him and the entire congregation of coders. The atmosphere inside the vast assembly hall changed immediately as the sound of typing fingers gave way to shocked silence.

The camera zoomed in on one of the dead cultists, revealing the Tarot card positioned right below the man's face. The card showed a skeletal knight in black armor astride a white horse, one hand holding up a black banner.

THE DEATH CARD.

Zagan struggled to make sense of the image.

Talon's raspy voice offered an explanation. *"Death is coming. For all of you..."* With this sinister promise, the screen went black.

CHAPTER TEN

THE DUCATI ROARED as Talon pulled onto Highway 101, headed for Silicon Valley. He didn't quite know what to expect as he closed in on the address Casca had texted him. What qualified as "home" for a billionaire moonlighting as an expert on the weird? Subconsciously he was expecting Wayne Manor, and the gated, sprawling estate didn't disappoint.

The electric gates whirred open and Talon entered the meticulously maintained grounds. He shot down the tree-lined, graveled driveway, past a foaming fountain and a stately garden. There was a beauty here but also a forlorn, deserted quality. Thousands of dollars were spent every month to tend to the property's natural beauty, without a soul around to enjoy it.

Talon killed his engine near the main entrance and parked beside the BMW. Moving swiftly, he mounted a series of stone steps that snaked toward the mansion. The two members of Casca's security team he'd sparred with earlier were waiting for him. Their faces remained unreadable but they kept a respectful distance as they escorted him into the lavish home.

"Sorry about the other day. No hard feelings, I hope," Talon said. He didn't want any resentment to fester now that he was working with the billionaire.

"Just part of the job." One of the guards winked; apology accepted. They led him down a wood-paneled hallway into a vast library. "Mr. Casca will be right with you."

The security guys left but the door remained open at his back. Talon studied the library. Recessed lights conjured moody shadows inside the museum-like chamber. For a moment he felt like he was back in the occult bookstore. The walls were either lined with ancient tomes or covered with an assortment of classical paintings. Talon marveled at a medieval depiction of beaming angels and red-skinned demons locked in an intense, existential battle.

The eternal conflict between good and evil raged on.

Talon's eyes landed on one of many glass display cases on the library floor. Each case contained exotic items capable of inspiring nightmares. There was an eerie voodoo doll. An obsidian skull. An assortment of cursed objects that Talon couldn't quite identify and wasn't sure he wanted to.

He stepped up to a case that held a leather-bound tome with strange, hieroglyphic-style writings. Talon scanned the illegible scribbling and became convinced that the dark letters hadn't been etched in ink, but human blood. His stomach roiled with revulsion as the irrational thought seized his mind. The book seemed alive, pulsing and oozing with raw, unnatural energy.

What made a man collect such morbid items? Was Casca just a bored rich guy, out to shock his well-heeled friends when they visited?

No, Talon knew there was a method behind the billionaire's madness, a reason for his obsession. Scanning the ancient depictions of heaven and hell, he wondered what demons drove his new benefactor.

"The Grimoire of the warlock Alexander Crowe." Casca's sudden appearance in the library startled Talon. Only rarely did someone manage to sneak up on him. This place was getting under his skin, dulling his normally razor-honed instincts.

"According to the legend, he inscribed his dark secrets in the blood of virgins."

"I bet it was a bestseller in its day," Talon said.

Casca raised an eyebrow. Talon winked. "You spoke with Becky?"

Casca nodded.

"What do you make of it?" Talon said.

"Omicron appears to be the cult's origin point."

Talon shook his head. "How is that possible? We're talking about a giant tech conglomerate here."

"How do you explain the mass suicides of the Jonestown massacre? Al Qaeda? ISIS? The dark power of any fringe organization comes from its message, and the conviction of its messenger."

"Who is this messenger?"   Talon said.

"That's for us to find out."

"What about the program Becky mentioned? The streaming of the murders?"

"Perhaps Omicron's program is the 21st Century answer to the Grimoire."

"Come again?" Casca had lost him.

"The warlock used the lifeforce of his victims to infuse the words on the page with occult power. Omicron might be developing a computer program that requires a similar level of sacrifice. Magic fueled by blood and suffering."

Casca's earnest tone gave Talon pause. He could feel his confusion growing. "I hope you don't actually buy into all this crazy stuff."

"Sergeant, do you know where the word 'occult' comes from?"

"Why do I have the feeling I'm about to find out?"

"It's Latin. The direct translation is 'knowledge of the hidden.' Secrets. There are mysteries in this world. Questions with no answers." Casca paused a beat before adding, "The dangers of the occult are real."

"And you're the guy who's going to save the world from the boogeyman?"

"Perhaps we can save it together."

Talon searched Casca's face and what he saw disturbed him. The man wasn't joking.

"You're serious about this, aren't you?"

The intensity in the billionaire's eyes answered the question far more eloquently than words ever could. "Come. Let's see what else Ms. Oakes can tell us about our enemy."

With these words Casca walked to the library's exit.

Talon followed.

***

The screen shimmered and undulated with streams of complex computer code. Hypnotic waves of data washed over Talon and Casca, painting their faces a bluish tint.

Seated in Casca's home office, they watched in expectant silence as Becky did her best to decipher the secrets of the dead cultist's laptop now resting on Casca's desk. The billionaire's office was both elegant and masculine, dominated by brown leather and burnished wood. Two armchairs faced an antique desk that probably cost more than most people's cars. A fireplace burned away in the corner, flickering flames bleeding crimson shadows across a number of classical sculptures and an illuminated globe. Detailed millwork added history to the timeless workspace.

Only thing missing is a box of cigars, Talon thought.

Studying Becky, he was surprised to see how quickly she'd recovered from her ordeal. The young woman was tough and determined to contribute in some way. Talon respected her fighting spirit. Even though Becky was an assistant she possessed a background in computer science and was certainly familiar with the Omicron product line. She might be able to help them gain a better understanding of the program these cultists were coding into existence.

"What are we looking at?" Talon asked.

"A piece of the larger program that these cult members are working on," Becky explained. "The code is designed to work with Omicron's Rapid framework and the large body of existing Objective-B programming language used by Omicron..."

Talon's eyes were already beginning to glaze over.

"There's something else going on here," Becky said. "Strange symbols unlike anything I've ever seen before."

Casca's eyes widened as he scanned the archaic text spliced between the lines of computer code.

"What do you make of it?" Talon asked.

"It's demonic, an ancient Egyptian script derived from the hieratic used in the Nile Delta."

"English, please," Talon said.

"Further study will be required before I can draw any definitive conclusions, but this code appears to contain incantations of some sort. Spells."

"At least it makes sense now." Talon fought the temptation to roll his eyes. They'd taken a sharp turn into the Twilight Zone. Flesh-and-blood fanatics were plotting their next horror while he wasted precious time with this nonsense. Talon steered the conversation back to the reality of the situation. "What do we know about Omicron and this Zagan character?"

"He's a rock star in his field," Becky said. Zagan's story was a myth within the halls of Omicron. Like most tech companies, Omicron believed in instilling an evangelical spirit in its workers. They were expected to internalize the goals of the company and sell its products to anyone they came in contact with. Knowing their CEO's history was part of their indoctrination.

"Zagan dropped out of college and worked for a series of videogame companies, as a coder. In an interview he described this period of his life as doing hard time inside a digital sweatshop. He quit EI-gaming and developed an app that went on to sell fifteen million copies. With the earnings, he started building Omicron and the rest is history."

Becky hit Google and photographs of Zagan flickered onscreen. The first shot showed him as a fresh college dropout, pudgy face half-concealed by a shaggy mop of hair. More photos popped up, showing how his style evolved as the years went by. The man began shaving his head to conceal a receding hairline and dropping the excess weight. Jeans and T-shirts gave way to thousand-dollar suits.

"Zagan reinvented himself over the last decade. As his fortune grew, so did the myth that has sprung up around him."

Talon compared the older shots with recent images of Zagan. The transformation was startling. His height and bone structure appeared to have undergone a radical metamorphosis.

"Hard to believe it's the same man," Casca said.

"Zagan likes to credit his rigorous workout regimen and strict Vegan diet for his new appearance. I'm not quite convinced."

Talon scrutinized Casca. The billionaire probably believed that dark magic was altering Zagan's body, but Talon refused to buy into such fairy tales. Money could purchase some pretty impressive plastic surgery. Sometimes success didn't banish demons; it merely fed them. Zagan was clearly trying to bury the memory of his old self.

"Here comes the million-dollar question — why does the head of one of the biggest computer companies in the Valley become a cult leader?"

"Good question. Hopefully I'll have an answer once I analyze this program more closely."

Talon didn't plan on sitting around idly while Casca cooked up some harebrained theory. Patience served its purpose in battle, but answering the Omicron call had been a declaration of war. In hindsight it was a foolish decision, perhaps, but burning rage had overruled cold logic. Zagan and his cult now knew that Talon was out there.

They were probably gearing up for a counterattack.

Talon would let Casca crack the code, if he wanted to. His preference was to receive an explanation for these killings, an explanation that came straight from Zagan's lips. Preferably followed by the dark thrill of pulling the trigger and sending the rotten bastard straight to hell.

"Alright guys, this was fun but I think it's time I

paid Zagan a little visit."

With these words, Talon stepped out of Casca's office. He barely made it down the next lavishly adorned hallway before the billionaire had caught up with him. Casca's eyes glittered with disapproval. "We should proceed with caution. We don't know what we're up against here."

"Maybe you don't, but I do. The CEO of Omicron is running his own killer cult. It's time someone stopped him before more innocent people end up dead."

"What's your plan? Walk into one of the biggest corporations in America and execute its leader?"

"If that's what it takes. We don't have the luxury of waiting around. They know we're closing in."

"What are you talking about?" Casca said.

Talon told the billionaire about the message he'd sent the cultists.

Casca shook his head. "You gave away our one advantage."

"Maybe I wanted to give these assholes a dose of their own medicine. Teach them what it means to be afraid."

"These fanatics don't fear you."

"They will."

"This isn't a game. You don't know what you're up against."

"I guess I'll find out."

"Talon, I know how much Michelle meant to you, and I know all too well what you're going through..."

Casca's familiar tone rubbed Talon the wrong

way and anger coiled in the pit of his stomach. "You have no clue how I'm feeling."

"Actually, I do." Casca's voice was cool and measured as he spoke. "Thirteen years ago, a cult of Satanists broke into this estate while my parents were celebrating their anniversary abroad. They killed the servants and took my sister and me hostage. Fortunately the FBI was nice enough to show up and shoot the bastards before I could become another statistic. My sister, unfortunately, wasn't so lucky."

Talon studied Casca more carefully. The boyish smile he usually wore didn't hint at this tragic past. The billionaire had found a way to hide the scars behind the easygoing facade he presented to the world. "So that explains all this?"

"My sister's death opened up my eyes to the dangers of the occult."

Casca stepped up to one of the large windows, moonlight casting him in an eerie light. "I know it's hard to wrap your head around all this, but if you hope to defeat Michelle's murderers you'll have to embrace a different reality. A reality most people would rather ignore. The supernatural and its agents of darkness are real."

"What the hell are you talking about?"

"Hell is *exactly* what I'm talking about." Casca's voice was trembling now, all pretense of cool gone. "You want to know my most horrible memory? Seeing a Satanist drive a knife into my sister's heart. Witnessing all life leaving her eyes. I could hear gunshots, the S.W.A.T. team fighting their way through the mansion… The Satanist turned toward me, my sister's blood still dripping from his blade. And that's when I saw *it*."

"Saw what?"

"Something that shouldn't exist. It was only for a split second but I knew it was real. Some entity that wasn't human had stepped into the sacrificial circle. It stood behind my sister's killer like a shadow — a creature not of this world. By the time help arrived and killed the Satanist, the entity had vanished. But I never forgot what I witnessed that day…"

Casca stared into the fire. "My nightmares won't let me."

Talon nodded. He understood a thing or two about nightmares. He'd seen too many good soldiers succumb to them. His friend Erik foremost among them.

Casca had endured a horrific trauma at an impressionable age. Talon didn't know what exactly the billionaire had experienced, but he was well aware of the mind's ability to conjure demons. Most people ran away from their nightmares. Talon liked to face them head on.

He'd identified the enemy.

It was time to go to war.

"I'm going to stop Zagan. You can help me, or you can get out of my way. It's your call."

Without saying another word, Talon walked out.

CHAPTER ELEVEN

THE GIANT VIEWING screen in the Omicron auditorium went dark. Zagan regarded his congregation of coders from behind the robotic skull-mask that had become as much a symbol of the cult as the binary number tattooed on each member's forearm.

For a moment, the crowd seemed frozen in tableau. Silently the programmers rose from their seats and left the auditorium. Tonight there wouldn't be a sacrifice. They instinctively sensed, like worker bees in a hive, that their task was complete.

Ten minutes later, only Zagan and four members of his security team remained in the empty assembly hall. He removed the robot mask and unceremoniously tossed it aside. His hands shook with rage, belying his otherwise calm exterior. Zagan drew comfort from the knowledge that the affront he'd witnessed would soon be repaid tenfold.

He turned to his head of security. Fisher was a former Marine with a face seemingly poured from concrete. "I want you to look into this. Find out who and what we're up against."

Fisher nodded before he and his men filed out. The head of security was reliable, a true believer.

Unlike Fisher, who was a staunch Satanist, Zagan didn't picture his master as a horned, biblical evil. He knew better.

Zagan's obsession with the occult had begun ten years before. Fresh out of college, he was a coder working for EI-Entertainment in Los Angeles. His initial excitement at landing a job at the company that had produced some of his most beloved videogames was soon crushed by the day-to-day reality of his new profession. Grueling twelve-hour days spent in a dark basement office/dungeon, slaving away at a computer, using his skill and talent to enrich men who didn't know he even existed.

A young Zagan had soon realized that he was just a blip in the Matrix, another geek with questionable social skills working in an office full of them.

But Zagan had dreams. Dreams of power. Dreams of revenge.

His new boss at EI, a bitter man named Peter Rice, seemed to be in some unspoken competition with every bully who'd ever pushed Zagan around. The man was petty, venal, exacting and loved to torment the programmers unlucky enough to wind up under his thumb. Zagan quickly became his favorite target. Rice would find fault where there was none, using any opportunity to criticize, humiliate and ridicule.

It took one day for Zagan to hate the man and one week before he wanted him dead.

Rice's systematic abuse was in a class of its own. He ruled the basement of EI-Electronics as if it was his personal fiefdom. Many times Zagan was tempted to quit, but a part of him refused to let the bully win.

A desire to turn his fate around burned bright inside of him. At night, Zagan would retreat into violent action movies and dark metal to numb himself. One of his favorites was *The Terminator*, especially the scene where Arnold cut a bloody swath through a bustling police precinct. The scene had ingrained itself into his imagination. How he wished he would have the guts to enter the basement at EI and unleash a volley of steel into his enemies, starting with Rice and his brown-nosing lackeys.

Zagan craved the strength of the fearsome killer cyborg. He yearned for a chance to realize his full potential.

A week later, fate would steer him toward his higher destiny. Zagan and the basement crew at EI were working on a game called *Hell World,* a *Doom* rip-off hoping to tap into the burgeoning military horror market. The design team had ordered stacks of research material, including a number of books on the occult and demonology.

The designers did all the creative heavy lifting; Zagan was just a coder who ironed out the kinks in the gameplay. There was no need for him to read any of these books, but something about the dark covers and cryptic titles spoke to him. During a bored lunch-break, Zagan skimmed one of the volumes.

What began with Zagan trying to stave off boredom turned into a marathon reading session. He stayed up all night and finished the first occult book. The next day he grabbed another volume and kept diving deeper into the mysteries contained within its pages. Most of the actual game creators barely glanced at the research materials, choosing to make stuff up instead of putting in the necessary research. Zagan, on the other hand, was hooked.

The books spoke of dark powers that man had learned to master, over the centuries. Devil. Satan. Abaddon. Shaitan. All names for the same evil energies that pulsed through the universe. Dark forces one could learn to channel, if the rituals outlined in the old texts were carefully followed.

As Zagan intensified his studies, a revolutionary idea occurred to him. What if by combining code and ancient ritual he could hack reality like a computer program? Voodoo was about to get a 21st Century upgrade.

The following night Zagan worked feverishly to write his occult program. It was a simple code modeled after an old racing game, but with a chilling twist. It incorporated magical ritual and information about Rice's brand-new Lexus. The program was designed to trigger a car accident in the real world.

When Zagan arrived at the office the next morning, Rice was already waiting for him. His vehicle was unharmed. Somewhere along the way, Zagan must've made a mistake.

Further research revealed the problem. For the code to exert its dark magic, it would require the lifeforce of a living creature. As this program's goals were modest, the sacrifice didn't have to be human. Nevertheless, blood would have to be spilled.

It didn't take Zagan long to find his victim. There was a stray cat that hung out around his shitty apartment complex. Using a bowl of milk, he lured the hungry feline into his unit. As soon as the poor animal lapped up the milk, Zagan threw a bag over its head. Without hesitation, he whipped out a kitchen knife and went to work on the hissing creature.

A minute later, his hands coated crimson, he started coding away. His bloody fingertips left dark imprints on the keyboard. His face covered in the dead animal's gore, he pounded the keys, a man possessed as he poured all his hatred, fear and rage into the program.

The following day his efforts would finally bear fruit. Rice's Lexus experienced a catastrophic failure when its four tires blew out at 80 mph on the freeway. Rice lost control of his Lexus and hit a median in a fiery explosion of metal, steel and flesh.

With the stroke of a few keys and one dead cat, Zagan's most ardent enemy had been erased from reality. It was his first taste of real power.

Over the next twelve months, Zagan created new programs. Some worked, some backfired. Each failure became a lesson, each success a hard-earned victory on the path to mastering the dark arts.

When he launched his first app a year later, he embedded occult code designed to persuade potential buyers to download it. The apps incredible success secured the financial foundation on which Omicron could be built.

With Zagan's rise to power, the programs grew more elaborate and complex. The years of experimentation had all led up to his latest brainchild — an occult reality-hacking program so grand and visionary it would put all his past efforts to shame. This latest code would assure Omicron's continued rise in the marketplace and allow him to crush his enemies.

Only a couple more sacrifices would be needed before his masterpiece was complete. Soon he would gain the ability to manipulate the physical world in ways his earlier self wouldn't dare to imagine.

But first this new problem would have to be dealt with. He'd worked too hard to let one tiny setback faze him. Whoever had killed his men would soon be experiencing the full power of Omicron's occult algorithm. The next stage of the plan was only hours away. Why not use the opportunity to draw out the enemy? As he sent out a series of texts to his followers, he made sure to include the cultists killed by the masked man.

Zagan was about to leave the auditorium when he experienced a sudden, sharp itch on his forearm. The binary tattoo had been strangely irritated for days now. He scratched the inked flesh and this time his nails came up red with blood. But it wasn't the sight of red that made his eyes light up. Under the bloody skin, rods of gray steel had replaced bone and muscle tissue.

Initial horror turned to dark wonder. He'd instructed the program to make him physically stronger, and the program was finding a way. Hacking reality. Changing him. Reshaping him into a creature as powerful as the cyborg from the future that had fired his imagination all those years earlier.

CHAPTER TWELVE

DETECTIVE JESSICA SERRONE blinked and shielded her eyes against the blinding sunlight as she walked up to the eco-house. Two uniformed officers stood guard at the front entrance. They exchanged quick greetings and stepped aside, granting her access. She didn't have to flash her badge, as the men recognized her.

Serrone wasn't someone you easily forgot. A German-Mexican heritage had given her both height and striking, exotic looks. Well-defined Aztec features projected a regal quality. Some of the less politically correct officers had started calling her Pocahontas behind her back. Serrone didn't mind. There were worse things than being nicknamed after a hot Disney princess.

Once inside the house, she approached the first body and tried not to disturb the team of forensics guys hard at work. Serrone spotted a knife next to the corpse. The dead man must've dropped it a second after his neck was snapped.

Another detective sidled up to her. With his ruddy features, Detective Nathan Grell formed a sharp contrast to Serrone's caramel complexion.

"Girlfriend of one of the stiffs called it in. Says he'd been acting a bit weird as of late. When she didn't hear from him last night, she got scared and let herself in. Two more guys upstairs. Hope you didn't have your breakfast yet. It gets gory once you reach the living room."

"Thanks for the warning."

Detective Serrone kneeled before the body. Longish hair and a goatee hid most of the dead man's acne scars. His wide-eyed stare seemed to follow her as she examined the body. She caught a glimpse of black ink on the victim's forearm – a series of ones and zeroes. She pulled back the sleeve and inspected the full sequence. By now she was familiar with the binary number. It had become the signature for these occult attacks. The only time she'd seen it outside of a crime scene was when they fished the three suicides out of the Bay.

The popular theory going around suggested that the tech workers had engaged in a murder-suicide pact. But now there were three more bodies. She somehow doubted this cult member had broken his own neck.

Serrone shifted her gaze to the latex robot mask. Talk about the perfect accessory for a murderous sci-fi cult. She made a quick mental note to track down suppliers that sold the masks in question.

"I guess Halloween came early this year. Think they got the three-for-one special?" Grell said.

Serrone didn't smile. This case was becoming more out there with each passing day. The cult theory had been initially met with skepticism. Serial killers were part of the mainstream nowadays, but cult killings veered into the weird and carried the whiff of homegrown terrorism. As the bodies kept piling up and the crimes grew more elaborate, her superiors couldn't ignore the mounting evidence.

The notion of a dark cyberpunk cult might sound fantastical, but it also made sense in a weird way to Serrone. San Francisco was a Mecca for anyone who wanted to make computers their career and possessed the technical talent to back up that ambition. A computer-science aesthetic would be a powerful hook for the designated target audience. Satanism, with its traditional occult trappings, was so last century. Binary numbers that spelled out 666 might be the kind of crazy twist on an old formula that would appeal to San Francisco's tech elite.

Serrone rose and followed Grell into the adjoining living room. A different scene awaited her in here. Blood speckled the plastic tarp spread out on the floor. The donors still wore their robot masks, one sporting a cyclopean eye where the round had entered. "Looks like these two were caught off guard. One was taken out by a headshot, the other fella appears to have offed himself. Nasty piece of business."

Serrone eyed the tarp. "They were interrupted. What I want to know is where's the victim and who's our vigilante with the itchy trigger finger?"

As she posed the question, a theory was already forming in her mind. The kills were clean, clinical. The work of a professional.

Perhaps the work of a Special Forces soldier out

for payback?

Her thoughts turned back to the shellshocked military man she'd faced in the interrogation room a few days earlier. When she first laid eyes upon Talon, she had experienced a disturbing sense of déjà vu. Her gut immediately pegged the shell of a man before her as a soldier. His hair was longish and his leather jacket and jeans were a far cry from military fatigues, but she couldn't shake the feeling. Maybe it was the way he carried himself or the intensity of his gaze, but on a subconscious level he reminded her of her Marine husband.

Bobby had been killed by an IED in Afghanistan, two years ago, leaving her a single mom with a young daughter that she was raising on her own. Even stranger was the simultaneous sensation that she was staring at herself. For months the same empty expression had gazed back at her from the mirror.

Losing Bobby hadn't merely signaled the loss of a lover and best friend but also the end of all her hopes for the future. She knew she might be projecting her own feelings onto the situation, but the memory of the grieving soldier had haunted her ever since.

His file was redacted, which suggested special ops. Possibly a Seal or Ranger. A professional warrior who'd returned from battle to spend time with someone he loved, only to realize death had followed him home.

Had Mark Talon chosen to take that pain and redirect it at the men who'd murdered his girlfriend?

It seemed like a far-fetched notion but the bodies sprawled on the floor told their own blood-soaked story. She made a mental note to pay Talon a visit. She was doubtful that anything would directly link the soldier to these murders, but maybe a part of her wanted to peer into those enigmatic eyes again. Did she secretly hope the ghost of her old lover might glance back at her once more?

Grell sidled up to her and pulled her back to reality. "Check this out."

Serrone followed him to a nearby computer workstation. The Omicron desktop was on and logged into Facebook. It showed an instant message: "*3 PM. Apple Store on Freemont. Hope to see you there.*"

Serrone realized that the message had come from a Facebook user named Jenna, a smiling twenty-something. Like the dead coders with the bloody Halloween masks, she worked in Silicon Valley. Had one of the victims been cheating on his girlfriend with this woman? Or could there be more to the meeting? Did the cult gather at Apple Stores to spread its wacky gospel and recruit new members?

"What do you make of it? Think it's related to this cult, or was roboboy breaking hearts online?"

"I don't know," Serrone replied. "It can't hurt to crash the party and see who shows up."

Had they finally caught a break in the case?

Serrone sure hoped so.

***

Talon's wish for a night unencumbered by nightmares was not to be. As soon as he closed his eyes, he was back in the barren mountains of Afghanistan. In the dream the Taliban fighters closing in on his position wore the skull-faces of robots and no matter how many rounds he pumped into the mechanical hordes, they just kept coming. Bullets tore into steel bodies, ripping out chunks of flesh wrapped in sizzling circuitry. The battlefield choked with the endoskeletons of the undying horde. For every inhuman fighter that succumbed to his firepower, another took its place.

The cybernetic terrorist army inexorably overran Talon's position and closed in for the kill. As a robotic hand snapped out at him, mechanical fingers closing around his throat, he was jolted from the apocalyptic nightmare.

Heart pounding, skin sheathed in sweat, the salt of his perspiration stinging his lips, he rose and checked the time. It was past ten o'clock. Despite the night terrors, he'd managed to get a few hours of sleep.

A new day awaited. A new battle.

For a second Talon wanted to ring Casca. Could he go it alone? Why had he turned his back on the billionaire? The answer was simple. Casca's beliefs in the supernatural made him question their partnership. An alliance had to be built on mutual trust; could he trust a man who thought demons and magic were real?

Talon showered and got dressed. He happened

to glance at the dead cultist's cell phone and homed in on the latest message. The sender was a girl named Jenna. She had sent the text about an hour after Talon put a bullet in its recipient's brain. *"3 PM. Apple Store on Freemont. Hope to see you there."*

Who was Jenna? Another member of the cult, or was this an unrelated gathering? It could be a trap, but it wasn't like this meeting was taking place in some deserted back alley. You couldn't find a more public place than an Apple Store if you tried. He was going to scout the Omicron campus regardless, and the Freemont Apple Store was only about ten minutes away.

He left the studio and spotted Erik washing his battered Mustang in the driveway. Talon took the man's willingness to take pride in his ride as a positive sign. Hopefully Erik was getting his act together.

"How goes the hunting?" Erik asked.

"It's started."

"Feel free to share."

Talon brought his buddy up to speed. He made it a point to leave out the occult program or the details surrounding Casca's past. When he got to the business of the Tarot card, Erik shook his head but couldn't wipe the wild grin off his face. "I bet they're starting to hate on you."

"About time."

Talon turned toward the Ducati and Erik touched his arm.

"Whatever you're up to, be careful."

"Ten years of playing in the terrorist sandbox, and I'm still here."

He winked at Erik with a cocky grin and cranked up the bike.

About an hour later he reached the Omicron campus. He parked his wheels and proceeded on foot. Circling the campus, he counted about 12 buildings interspersed with green spaces. He passed a running track, a gym and a vast cafeteria. The only area open to the public was the company store.

As he sauntered past the main building, he inspected the security guards posted in the lobby. He counted four men fronting the main desk. Getting to Zagan would be a challenge, but not impossible. He'd find a way. After another hour of navigating the campus, Talon wrapped up his reconnaissance and headed for the his next stop.

It was about five minutes before three when he closed in on the Apple store and spotted a familiar face: Detective Jessica Serrone. Immediately he turned away, shielding his features before she could spot him.

Taking a few steps back, Talon planted himself next to a tree and kept his head low. Behind the store's glass wall, a male detective trailed Serrone. They knew about the text message, Talon realized, but didn't quite know what they should be on the lookout for.

That makes two of us, Talon thought.

Inside the store the iPads, iPhones and various other Apple products were fully on display in the high-ceilinged, brightly lit venue. The multiplicity of screens flashed and flickered with the promise of progress. Blue-shirted salespeople offered helpful advice and scanned credit cards with the their smartphone apps. From his position Talon couldn't quite make out the Genius Bar and the classroom area. His gut told him that any meeting would be taking place in the back of the store.

Nothing was setting off any of his alarm bells. Yet. What had he expected? Watching Serrone as she navigated the crowds, he recognized a similar disappointment on her face. The text message lead had turned into a bust.

Talon tilted his head to his motorcycle... and that's when the world descended into madness.

CHAPTER THIRTEEN

DETECTIVE SERRONE NAVIGATED through the bustling Apple Store, Grell at her side. Her eyes were roving but she didn't know what to expect or look for. According to the text, the dead cultist was supposed to meet someone at the store at three o'clock, but the how and why remained a mystery. Jessica marveled at the latest iPhone model and realized she was way past due for an upgrade. Her four-year-old phone had officially attained fossil status.

Grell nodded sagely, as if he could read her mind. "You need to get a new phone, kid." Grell was a self-proclaimed gadget freak and wouldn't be caught dead with outdated tech.

"My phone works fine," Jessica said.

"Your phone is disturbing to me and all these good people working here."

"I can send texts and make phone calls. Do I need anything else?"

"You're an old soul," Grell concluded.

Maybe I'm a single mom raising her seven-year-old daughter on a cop salary, Serrone thought, but kept her mouth shut. Grell meant well.

Serrone approached the Genius Bar as it turned three. Friendly, smart men and women in blue shirts manned the long table, offering help to the never-ending parade of customers. Serrone's gaze lingered on the logo of the three electrons orbiting an atom – strange that she'd never paid attention to it before.

To her left was a small space reserved for teaching a variety of workshops. It was deserted except for the elderly gentleman catching his breath in one of the empty chairs.

Jessica battled her sense of disappointment and chewed her lower lip, a bad tick she'd developed since the death of her husband. Had she truly expected to stumble upon a secret cult meeting in a bustling retail store? She cursed herself for having wasted their precious time with this nonsense. Judging from the sour expression on her partner's face, he must've come to the same dour conclusion.

"Everything seems pretty normal."

"No shit."

Jessica circled the store one more time, her eyes taking in each patron, analyzing every detail about them. There was a young female college student with curious eyes and way too many piercings; a middle-aged African-American male with dreads; a stylishly decked-out gay couple in their late twenties. The faces after a while became a blur, a cross-section of America. Most of them were well-dressed, enthusiastic, filled with excitement and curiosity about the abundance of technological marvels surrounding them.

Serrone was about to call it a day when her face

stared back at her from one of the iMacs. Someone had switched on the computer's webcam. Her gaze roamed the store and spotted a customer switching on webcams, one after another.

Strange.

She turned, eyes scoping. Everywhere the scene repeated itself. She counted about thirteen people making the rounds, moving from desktop to desktop, laptop to laptop, iPad to iPad, iPhone to iPhone in an eerie quest to activate the cameras on all the devices. The maneuver seemed weirdly synchronized and choreographed, almost as if the customers involved were communing with one another on a telepathic level.

What's going on here?

Serrone's stomach tightened with a dawning realization. All these people must've received the same text message. The insight triggered two words.

Flash mob.

As soon as the idea occurred to her, the first of the suspicious customers whipped out a six-inch blade and drove it into a blue-shirted sales person.

***

Talon's pulse quickened as the knife plunged into the unsuspecting man's back and his blue shirt turned red. Shock gave way to pain and the man's lips distorted into a scream. The knife went in again and again. This was the beginning of the horror. More customers pulled out blades and stabbed the people closest to them. Knives flashed and found soft flesh.

At the center of the savagery stood Serrone and her partner. They drew their firearms and a second later, a bullet bounced off the Apple Store's storefront window, spiderwebbing its bulletproof surface.

The rising tide of violence galvanized Talon into action. He donned his balaclava mask and pulled the Glock from his shoulder holster. An instant later, he powered through the store's front entrance. To his right blood geysered from a knife wound and hit the 15-inch MacBook Pro. As he advanced, his image mirrored him on the various computer screens like a digital shadow.

A chill jolted down Talon's spine. The webcams were on and streaming the bloodbath online. Were coders less than two miles away working on their twisted occult program?

Rage boiled up as he leveled his Glock and stopped one knife-wielding assailant with a clean shot to the shoulder. Blood sprayed. The impact made the attacker drop the red-stained blade, but he barely responded to the wound.

There was no time to ponder this eerie phenomenon as another cultist rushed him, a big man who carried as much muscle as flab. The man moved fast for someone lugging his bulk. Sharp steel slashed the air, coming up fast. Talon snatched a nearby laptop and blocked the incoming blade. The impact rattled the keyboard, traveling up his arms. Once, twice, before he whipped the laptop right across the attacker's face. The man's head snapped back as Talon brought the computer full-force down on his head. The fat man crumpled like a downed mastodon.

Talon spun around. There were so many attackers, so much blood, that it became hard to distinguish friend from foe. For a second he felt like he'd stepped into a zombie flick.

The freakiest part for Talon was the utter lack of emotion driving the cruelty. The faces of the knife-wielding killers remained expressionless. However, their eyes shone with a merciless fanaticism. An army possessed.

Talon targeted knees and arms, disabling the mad horde as best he could. Something about the inhuman fanaticism fueling the attacks made him hold back and not use lethal force. He couldn't shake the feeling that these people weren't in control of their actions. For a moment he almost wished there was some sort of supernatural explanation for this madness.

A bestial shriek cut through the Apple Store as another man tried to tackle Talon. He felled the fanatic before the tip of his knife could run him through.

The Apple Store had become a warzone, recalling the crazed aftermath of a suicide bombing. The smoke of gunfire clouded the air and the screams took over. The wounded and dying were everywhere – employees, cultists and customers.

He spotted Serrone. For a beat their eyes met across the devastation inside the Apple Store. Her gaze reflected terror and shock. Her partner's body lay slumped to her side, hemorrhaging red.

Talon grew still as a fanatic rose behind Serrone. He clutched the hilt of his blood-caked blade with both hands, about to plunge it deep into her back.

Talon squeezed the trigger and half the fanatic's face erupted in a bloody cloud. Brain splattered a 5k Retina display as the impact spun the man around in a grotesque pirouette. He collapsed in a lifeless heap.

Serrone lowered her weapon, knowing the masked man's quick action had saved her life and turned toward her downed partner. Grell gasped and exhaled blood. Sirens keened in the near distance and a crowd was gathering at the front entrance. Any moment now cops would pour through those doors and another kind of hell would erupt.

Talon needed to get out of here. Now.

As he scanned for a rear exit, he spotted one of the knife-wielding attackers melting into the background. This man was making his getaway. He traded a final glance with Serrone before rushing past her, sprinting after the last fanatic.

The man vanished through the back door and Talon stayed right on his ass. Seconds later, they were out in the store's back parking lot, the sun baking down on them.

His quarry slowed his gait and dropped the bloody knife between two parked cars. The man was doing his best to blend in with the gathering crowd of curious onlookers.

Talon followed his example, having removed his

mask seconds before stepping into the lot. He moved briskly, eyes on point, never losing track of the target navigating his way through the throng.

The cultist advanced toward a white Tesla. Talon waited for him to slip into the driver's seat before he opened the passenger door and got inside. The bore of Talon's Glock dug into the man's chest.

"Drive."

The man slowly complied. Not every Jihadist was a suicide bomber and the same held true for these cultists - this fanatic came with a will to live. A plan was forming in Talon's mind. And this guy would help him carry it out.

Talon had been looking for a way into Omicron. He'd found it.

CHAPTER FOURTEEN

THE CULTIST KEPT his eyes on traffic, all too aware of the gun pressed against his ribcage. One wrong move and he was history. Ten minutes had passed since the vicious attack on the Apple Store. Odds were good that the coders might still be inside the auditorium, drawing inspiration from their twisted muse. A perfect opportunity to drop by and share some quality time.

Talon palmed the cultist's Omicron identification badge. His name was Richard Webb. "So tell me, Richard, what goes through a crazy person's head? Are you like, 'man I'm a psychotic fruit loop, today is a beautiful day to go stab some innocent people?'"

"We mock that which we don't understand."

"A true believer, huh? I wonder what your leader will have to say when he finds out you didn't have the guts to off yourself like the others."

"We all serve in our own way."

A nervous shiver rippled through Richard's features and Talon smiled. The enemy hiding behind the robot masks was all too human.

"Turn right."

Richard did as he was told and the Omicron campus jumped into view. They drove into the parking structure and Talon commanded Richard to swipe his badge. The security gate rose, offering them full access.

Richard parked the car as instructed. Talon grabbed the cultist by the collar and kept the gun trained on him as they both got out of the Tesla on the passenger side. There was a bank of elevators about forty feet away. An empty chair flanked the steel lift, but there was no sign of a guard. "How many guards are in the lobby?"

"About four."

Not an ideal scenario, but it could've been worse.

Talon didn't know who belonged to this cult and who didn't. He wasn't eager to kill any innocent bystanders.

"Walk next to me. Pretend we're having a wonderful conversation. If you do anything fishy, I'll shoot you. If you call for help, I'll blow your fucking brains out. Got it?"

Richard nodded and swiped the card. The elevator doors split open. Seconds later, the lift ascended.

Talon studied his hostage and wondered what could have pushed him into this madness. *The dark power of any cult comes from its message*, Casca had said. But what was the message here? How could such fanaticism find fertile soil in the homeland?

The elevator door zoomed open. They stepped

out onto the ground level. A cathedral of glittering glass and brushed steel awaited them. Exotic plants abounded, creating the illusion of walking through a giant greenhouse. Could this tranquil environment truly harbor a killer cult?

It boggled Talon's mind.

Ahead of them, Talon took note of the guards. Four men wearing suits and ear-mics manned the security desk. This would be the tricky part.

Richard flashed them a quick smile and the guards didn't pay any more attention to them. He was just another worker returning from a long lunch.

Richard was playing ball. *Smart man.* Seeing his buddy's brain splattered on an iMac like a Jackson Pollock painting had left a lasting impression.

They crossed the atrium-sized space of the main lobby. Talon caught glimpses of the upstairs offices, the glass walls putting them on display as if they were all inside a big aquarium. For a beat he wondered if the cult membership came with Omicron shares and a medical plan. Talon smiled grimly. Nice to know his dark sense of humor was intact. It had helped him through some tough patches over the years.

Talon spotted more powerfully built guards fronting the auditorium's main entrance. Remembering that Becky mentioned a back door leading to the assembly hall's balcony, he ordered Richard to show him the way. They closed in on a glass elevator that was tinted blue. A minute later they got out on the second floor and headed for a door located at the end of the hallway.

Richard swiped his security card and the door swung open. The moment they stepped inside, Talon rammed the butt of his Glock against the back of Richard's head. The cultist slumped to the ground, down for the count.

For a second, Talon considered his next move. His stomach churned with uncertainty. It almost felt too easy but he'd come too far to turn back. He shot a final glance at Richard's unconscious form and moved deeper into the darkness.

Body coiled and gun up, he advanced toward the edge of the balcony overlooking the cavernous amphitheater below. About 80 of the 300 seats were occupied with coders. They faced the screen and its images of violence with hushed, religious awe. Cameras streaming images from the store, the programmers kept tapping their keyboards while cops and emergency workers rushed back and forth on the giant screen. The scene reminded Talon of the aftermath of a battle. He rapidly scanned the streaming images for Serrone but saw no sign of the detective. Talon's eyes shifted from the screen to the man who commanded this unholy gathering.

Zagan.

Their leader fronted his audience, a magnetic presence in his robot skull mask. Talon sighted the man with his Glock. He was about to squeeze the trigger when Zagan fixed his gaze on the balcony. Almost as if he could detect Talon in the dark...

As if to confirm this suspicion the jumbo screen went black and filled with a new, even more shocking image. Talon's blood turned to ice as he took in the new feed. A familiar face stared up at him, blood staining broken teeth, hair matted crimson. It was his friend Erik, cultists hovering at the edges of the frame, knives out.

Zagan's voice rang out. "Welcome, Sergeant Talon. So nice of you to join us."

CHAPTER FIFTEEN

TALON'S FINGERS TIGHTENED around the grip of his Glock. He'd walked into a trap! The cultist playing along, the relative ease in getting past the guards – it was all part of a well-orchestrated charade. His thirst for revenge had blinded him to the reality that should've been obvious. He'd underestimated the enemy, and now both he and Erik were about to pay a steep price for his carelessness.

How did Zagan know his name? How had he connected him to Erik?

He pushed these questions aside and allowed his body to jump into action. The gun came up as the first knife closed in on Erik.

Oh God, not again...

Talon's helpless rage detonated. Driven by pure reflex, he sighted down on Zagan and emptied a full magazine into the man. The hail of bullets caught the Omicron CEO in the throat and forehead, whipping his head back in a cloud of blood. The cult leader went down hard.

Talon slammed a new magazine into his Glock

and left the balcony with quick strides. He tore past an unconscious Richard, fighting back the temptation to finish off the fanatic. He'd need every bullet he had if he was going to fight his way out of the Omicron complex.

Talon burst through the exit and sprinted down the long passageway, eyes scanning his fishbowl surroundings. Armed security people approached from the other side of the atrium, guns ready.

He had to get out of here and contact Casca. Maybe Erik might still have a chance if help arrived on time. Bypassing the elevators, he headed for a nearby exit that led to the stairs. Moving, moving. He pushed through the door and found himself...

Back in the auditorium.

For a moment the world tilted and shifted and unhooked from reality. He'd covered about two hundred feet, so how could the door at the far end of the hallway lead him right back to where he started?

Erik's terrified features filled the mammoth screen. Shifting his gaze away from the scene, it landed on Zagan who had risen to his feet again. The cult leader was still alive?!

Impossible.

For a second Talon's training failed him and terror seized hold of his mind. There had to be a rational explanation for what he was experiencing. They must have drugged him somehow. Maybe slow-acting toxin, most likely airborne, had filtered into the balcony through the ventilation system.

Who was he kidding? The theory didn't sound

convincing. Casca's voice drowned out his halfhearted attempt at rationalizing the impossible.

The supernatural and its agents of darkness are real.

A meltdown wasn't going to help him get out of this predicament. He fought the fear and replaced it with anger directed at Michelle's murderers who'd now gone after his friend too. Not knowing what else to do, Talon stormed out of the auditorium, rushing down the passage once again. Instead of heading for the staircase this time, he kept on going. He made a sharp left turn and... stared down a corridor stretching into infinity.

Reality whiplashed.

Talon pivoted and was confronted with another endless hallway with no end in sight. The hallways extended endlessly before him, the entire building transformed into a surreal maze that would make M. C. Escher jealous.

Desperately trying to blink away the madness, Talon staggered toward the nearest elevator. In the distance, he spotted a phalanx of fast-approaching figures. Omicron's security team. He leveled his Glock and froze...

Another impossible sight raked his sanity and strangled all thoughts. He knew these guards, had served with them, fought with them. He'd seen them die.

Zagan's security team was made up of his fallen comrades in arms. On his right was Sgt. McComery. Killed by a sniper bullet in Fallujah. To his left, Robert J. Walker. Torn apart by a roadside bomb on the dusty roads of Kabul. At the center of the undead trio was one of his closest friends, Michael Dugan, who'd taken a bullet meant for Talon and succumbed to his wounds in the stark mountains of Afghanistan. Was he going insane?

His fallen brothers-in-arms raised their firearms and locked in on him.

Talon hesitated. It's a trick, an illusion...

Bullets punched the air and Talon automatically returned fire. Lead ripped into the guards wearing his dead friends' faces. Talon stifled a scream as he felt the impact of each bullet on his own body. He looked down at his chest and saw blood oozing from ragged holes in his torso.

Talon spit blood and turned away from the dead guards, the once-again lifeless eyes of his old friends haunting him. Under his feet, the shiny floor shifted and undulated, distorting and changing texture. It was turning syrupy as physical reality turned against him. With each successive step, he sank deeper into the swamp-like floor.

Talon's gaze became wild, ticking back and forth in a frenzied attempt to make sense of his warping reality.

Another figure appeared. The master of this nightmare. Zagan.

The Omicron CEO loomed before Talon, now an impossibly tall, otherworldly presence, strangely distorted as if Talon was viewing him through a funhouse mirror. The man tore off his robot mask to reveal the gaping holes where Talon's bullets struck him earlier. Under the gory skin, Talon saw glimpses of silver gray that hinted at a metallic death skull lurking behind the flesh-and-blood façade.

The man had become the mask; the mask was becoming the man.

A second later, the swirling floor engulfed Talon, erasing the world in darkness.

CHAPTER SIXTEEN

THEY CALLED HIM the devil soldier.

Zagan's head-of-security, Fisher, had earned the nickname in Fallujah when his Marine division came under heavy fire. With the casualties in his unit mounting, Fisher started praying. First to God, but the Almighty refused to answer his calls for help. All around him, bullets kept felling good men. The dust of the desert city turned red with their blood.

Desperate, his fury growing, Fisher kept whispering new prayers. Prayers directed at the Prince of Lies.

Thirty minutes later, reinforcements arrived in the besieged city and the tide of war turned. As superior firepower tore the Iraqis apart, Fisher switched his allegiance to a new master.

Stumbling through the battlefield, bleeding from various wounds, his skin baking in the desert heat, he sought out his enemy. He found one bullet-ridden Iraqi, head held high despite his sorry state. His defiance dissolved into an expression of agony as Fisher sunk his Ka-Bar into the man's throat.

As the Iraqi soldier perished in the blood-soaked dust, Fisher pledged the fallen enemy's soul to his dark savior. Later that evening, he stripped off his armor and fatigues and, using his Ka-Bar, he carved a pentagram into his chest.

It was a token of his newfound devotion to the forces of darkness.

Within a year he received a dishonorable discharge for his actions. Fisher worked odd jobs when he returned to San Francisco, mostly as a bouncer in seedier nightclubs. His chance for redemption came when Zagan hired him as his head-of-security.

Almost immediately he felt a kinship with his new employer. They both served the same dark master, in their own ways. Consequently, Omicron's new enemy was his enemy. Fisher promised to make the masked man who'd slaughtered three true believers pay dearly for his insolence.

The brazen attack, as well as the willingness to take lives and resort to guerilla tactics, indicated the work of a fellow professional. The ferocity of the Tarot warning suggested a personal vendetta.

This assassin must be connected to one of the victims, Fisher thought.

His next step was to review the cult's recent victims. Michelle's soldier boyfriend jumped out at him from the start. The photographs of Mark Talon that accompanied the reports of Michelle's murder gave him a bad feeling. The man's hollow gaze spelled trouble to Fisher's battle-hardened mind.

This was a foe to be reckoned with. He needed to learn more about the man and his relationship with Michelle.

Fortunately, they still had the reporter bitch's laptop.

A few hours after Talon sent his declaration of war, Fisher was going through Michelle's email accounts. He quickly located her correspondence with Talon. It painted a pretty clear picture of their intense relationship and also provided clues as to what sort of man Omicron was up against.

Fisher's eyes lit up at the mention of Delta. This wasn't some cowboy with a death wish but one of the best-trained military men in the world. A true challenge.

Fisher loved a challenge.

Perusing the emails, another name kept popping up. Erik. A friend of Talon's who lived in Oakland. Was Talon holing up with his old war buddy? Only one way to know for sure... Fisher palmed his phone and alerted the security team. There was work to be done.

The next day, he pulled up to Erik's rundown Oakland home. He told the three members of his crew to stay in the car while he scoped out the property. Erik's freshly washed car was still drying in the early afternoon sun as he snuck into the yard. Unbeknownst to him, he'd missed Talon by just thirty minutes.

He scanned the weed-infested backyard and spotted a shadowy shape flitting past the window. Someone appeared to be home. Good. He hugged the side of the house. Advancing with caution, he located the guesthouse in the back.

An instant later Fisher was picking the guesthouse door's lock. It opened with a rasp and he breached Talon's makeshift command center. One glance at the occult literature splayed out on the wooden desk convinced him that he'd come to the right place.

Curiosity piqued, he checked the laptop and scanned its history. Articles on Omicron abounded. There were also a few stories about a Silicon Valley billionaire by the name of Simon Casca. *Interesting.* He would have to review this information more carefully and let Zagan know about Casca. First though they would deal with the man in the house.

He drew his cell and contacted the team. "We're going in."

***

The bottle was calling him.

Erik's promise of sobriety was crumbling. Everywhere he turned, reminders of his addiction screamed out at him. Crushed beer cans. Empty whiskey bottles. He had wisely poured out all the booze in the house... Except for the flask he kept stashed in his parents' bedroom. He had spared it for a moment like this.

A moment when the overpowering thirst would come.

As he climbed the stairs, Erik's tongue flicked over his lips in growing anticipation. He could already taste the liquid's warming sting.

One drink.

One drink wouldn't hurt anyone.

He thought that helping Talon would defeat his demons. But Talon wasn't involving him in his new mission in any substantial way. Talon might claim he was being protective, but Erik knew the truth. Talon didn't trust him. The soldier he once was now buried under too much booze and bad food.

I'm useless. Dead weight. And Talon knows it.

The thought brought back all the old feelings of guilt and self-hatred. His somber mood weighed on him. But it was nothing a stiff drink (or two) couldn't cure. It would clear out the bad wiring. Get him back on track.

Erik was about to climb the stairs and give in to his addiction when he heard a noise from outside. It sounded like someone was at his back entrance. Was someone attempting to burglarize his place?

He stole a quick glance through the bedroom window and spotted two men picking the lock outside. In their suits and shades, the two would-be intruders reminded him more of Feds than any of the local neighborhood punks.

A dark realization edged into his awareness. Talon's new enemies had found them.

Erik ran through his options.

His first instinct was to go for his Glock. Unfortunately, Talon had his gun. Calling the cops would be the next logical move, but his cell was downstairs in the living room. Probably buried on his couch somewhere. Shit.

140

He could wait for these guys to break into his house, or he could make a run for the phone. He might even have enough time to snatch a knife from the kitchen cupboard.

Storming down the stairs, he realized he wasn't afraid and his thirst was gone. A different Erik was in the driver's seat now. This Erik had fought off six armed Iraqis with only a bare knife. He had commanded the respect of his unit. This Erik had been a man Talon was proud to call his friend.

Welcome back, brother.

He had barely reached the foot of the stairs when the front door swung open and two men stormed into his home. In his mind, Erik felt like a soldier again, but his body sagged under the last few years of self-abuse. He couldn't generate the same speed and power when he threw the first punch and missed his target by a wide margin.

Unfortunately his opponents were trained professionals. It all happened so fast. Before he knew it Erik was sprawled on his dusty, stained carpet.

A boot kicked him in the mouth, followed by the coppery flavor of his blood. More kicks came in quick succession, landing against a belly turned to mush. He hunched over, gasping for air. But he didn't scream. There was still no fear. He'd been waiting to meet his maker for quite some time now.

Erik had lost count of how many times he'd considered eating a bullet. The sole reason he'd never gone through with it was his mom. He wouldn't want the world to think Mrs. Garrison had raised a quitter.

Erik had a pretty good idea what was going to happen next. He was ready.

Bring it on, you bastards!

The big man in the group of home invaders — Erik instantly pegged him as military — nodded to his men. The youngest member of the group, a punk who couldn't be older than twenty or so, approached Erik. Knife out.

Let's see if the kid has it in him, Erik wondered.

Steel flashed and descended in a hypnotic arc. Sharpened metal sliced through two years of junk food and booze.

The little fucker actually has the cojones to stick a man — look at this shit!

The area where the blade had entered felt cold, but Erik experienced no pain. At least not yet. Wasn't adrenaline wonderful? The wound felt almost like being stung by a bee. The kid registered no emotion as he hovered above him. His bland indifference gave Erik the necessary kick to respond and probably explained what he did next.

Erik's fingers closed around the knife in his belly and pulled it out of his flesh. He saw shock in the young man's face, which deepened when the same knife sliced open his thigh in a stream of red.

The cultist stumbled aside with a cry of pain.

Erik grinned and in that moment he was back in Iraq, nineteen years old. Young, dumb and full of cum. Ready to face any enemy and endure any hardship. The moment was shattered seconds later as more blades went to work on him, but it allowed

Erik to flash a bloody grin at the cameras recording his remaining moments.

"I hope Talon sends every one of you bastards to hell," he hissed before all strength left his bleeding body and blackness claimed him.

CHAPTER SEVENTEEN

TALON DRIFTED THROUGH the void. An impenetrable blackness, defined by a perfect silence that was finally broken by a familiar voice. *"The dangers of the occult are real."*

The billionaire's words pierced the silence. It drove home a truth that was growing more pervasive in his mind. Zagan wasn't like any opponent he'd faced before.

You're in way over your head, kid.

His refusal to pay heed to Casca's wisdom would now cost him dearly. Ignoring intelligence on the battlefield carried with it dire consequences.

Without warning, the darkness lifted. Waves of phosphorescent green light engulfed him. Talon was back in Omicron's assembly chamber. He was bare-chested and tied to a chair facing the stage. Zip-ties cut into his wrists.

The vast screen was unspooling Erik's final moments once more, a terrible, sickening loop. As Erik's screams reverberated throughout the cavernous auditorium, Talon jerked against his restraints, shaking with rage. *"You fucking cowards, I'll kill you all!"*

Talon craned his neck and spotted a small army of computer programmers seated in the rows behind him. Fingers drilled the keys of their laptops, blank eyes in the thrall of some ungodly spell. How could so many people remain indifferent to the violence onscreen?

"I see you're awake, Sergeant. Good."

Talon spun toward the direction of the voice. Zagan lurked in the shadows, a silhouette outlined against the flickering screen. He stepped into the light, his ascetic features coming into view. The knife in Zagan's hand promised Talon a painful, drawn-out end.

Talon steeled himself for the torture ahead. To meet death in battle was different than being captured by the enemy and becoming their helpless plaything. Any man could be broken, and Talon held no illusions that he would prove the exception to that rule. Nevertheless, he met Zagan's gaze without flinching.

"Years ago, I worked on a first-person shooter called *Hell World*," Zagan said. "It featured soldiers battling demons. Pretty cutting-edge for its day. In the game, the military always defeated the hordes of hell. Too bad we're not playing a game, huh?"

Zagan took a step closer. Talon strained against his ropes. They didn't budge. "I know you're working with someone. Behind every good soldier is a great general pulling the strings. Someone has been helping you." He paused for a moment before asking, "Who is Simon Casca?"

"I'd be careful with that knife. You might poke

your eye out."

"Sill cracking jokes in the face of defeat?"

"I have a hard time taking anyone seriously who wears a Halloween mask."

Zagan stopped his advance for a beat. His smile was now replaced with a flicker of anger. Good. Perhaps if he played his cards right and provoked Zagan enough, the Omicron CEO would kill him and skip the torture.

"I know what you're trying to do, but it won't work. You've seen firsthand what my program can do. Soon I'll be able to manipulate reality like no one has ever done before."

"Maybe try to fix male-pattern baldness, for a start. Might do wonders for your look."

Zagan's hand shot out at Talon's throat, fingers digging into his windpipe. Up close, Talon caught a full view of where his bullets had struck the man. Or was Zagan still a man at all? Steel shimmered inside the wounded tissue. What was the Omicron CEO turning into?

"I'm changing," Zagan explained, almost as if he could read Talon's thoughts. "Growing stronger with each sacrifice."

Talon gasped for air.

"Each kill."

Zagan released him and Talon struggled for air. He was still sucking in gulps of precious oxygen when Zagan dug the point of the knife into his bare chest. Talon's muscles tensed against the assault and his lungs bellowed with agony.

"The best way to defeat someone is to make

them serve you."

Talon screamed more with rage than pain as Zagan drew the slicing edge over his chest. Another cultist filmed his ordeal and streamed it to the assembly hall's viewing screen. These bastards were coding away to the accompaniment of his personal agony.

I'm going to kill every one of you fucking assholes, Talon thought as he gnashed his teeth with fury. The meaty stench of blood impregnated the air. He felt its warmth streaming down his exposed torso.

Zagan proceeded with his grisly work, inflicting one cut after another. Talon's bare skin had become the canvas for Zagan's madness. Blood dripped down Talon's mutilated torso, staining his pants. Zagan kept slicing away with precision and a focused intent.

A minute later Zagan took a step back to inspect his handiwork. Talon peered up at his own battered image. His torso hemorrhaged an inverted pentagram. The bastard had branded him!

"I'll kill you."

"Oh, you're wrong about that, Talon. You'll serve me. You'll serve the darkness. Sooner than you think."

The cultist with the cam zoomed in until the inverted star on Talon's chest completely filled the giant screen. A beat later, the image was replaced with roiling streams of code. The occult algorithm.

Talon averted his gaze but the waves of code seemed to pursue him like the floating images in a

3-D movie. Rising tides in a digital ocean. Once again, reality had ceased to obey the laws of physics.

Help me!

Memories fused with the supernova of data streaming through his brain. Sanity buckling despite his best efforts, Talon struggled to cling to something tangible, something real that would ground him.

War had taught him not to waste precious energy obsessing over details that were beyond his control. It was a lesson he'd learned during an Alpine mountain climbing exercise. He foolishly hazarded a glance upward and literally realized his whole life dangled on a six-inch metal spike. Panic gripped him. Fortunately one of his climbing instructors pulled him aside him and told to him to narrow his reality to a three-foot radius. The message was clear; he should live his life trying to affect what was within three feet of him and nothing else. Focus on that which you can control and ignore the rest.

Easier said than done.

Applying the philosophy, Talon concentrated on his breathing. He inhaled through his nose for a count of four... Held his breath for four seconds... The point was to breathe deeply and methodically, completely filling and emptying his lungs during each cycle. The technique worked somewhat, but the data floating around him remained. With each inhalation, he breathed in the program. Line after line of code. His frame convulsed.

Someone make it stop. Please, make it stop!

All thoughts ceased. His reality was reduced to the shining vision of an inverted pentagram, which now hovered on the giant screen before him. A beacon showing him a new way. A path toward redemption. Toward the darkness.

Talon never felt Zagan's men cut his zip-ties, never experienced his body rising and straightening as he slipped his jacket over his bloody chest.

Never saw Zagan lean into him.

All he remembered were the words his new master whispered into his ear. "Kill your general."

CHAPTER EIGHTEEN

IMAGES OF THE Apple Store massacre flickered over Simon Casca's 90-inch plasma-TV screen. His stomach churned as he sat in his office and absorbed the horrific story. Casualty numbers kept being adjusted, but at least eleven people were dead and an equal number were in critical condition. Video of the attack dominated all the major news networks. This was a global case now and speculation ran rampant as to the identity and agenda of the killers. Terrorism was on everyone's lips, but Casca knew better. Zagan's cult had struck again.

Footage of a masked rescuer suggested that Mark Talon had crashed Omicron's party. God, how Casca wished the Delta operator would return his calls. The bloodbath at the Apple Store confirmed his worst fears. The actions of this killer cult were escalating.

Casca turned off the news and shifted his attention back to his desk. The cultists' laptop was running the program segment and eerie streams of code slithered over the screen. Becky had assisted him all day long, but she was now asleep in one of the estate's many spare bedrooms. Analyzing the incomplete code had offered invaluable insights into the challenge they faced. It was far worse than expected. The world was in terrible danger.

For years Casca had anticipated a devastating occult attack. Reports of global occult activity were popping up on a daily basis. Warlords indulging in voodoo, biker gangs and drug cartels practicing satanic rituals, South American cartels tapping into Santeria... The list went on. Small, isolated incidents that when added up could produce a disturbing cumulative effect. It didn't bode well for the future.

And now this computer cult had arrived seemingly out of nowhere. In Casca's mind, it represented the greatest threat he'd faced so far.

The billionaire stifled a yawn and downed his fourth Americano of the night. His body and mind protested, craving sleep, but there was no time for rest.

Casca decided to stretch his legs and go for a quick walk through the vast occult library adjacent to his office. His muscles ached and the physical activity might ease his anxiety. There was something terrifying about being here late at night, but Casca drew a strange comfort from the creepy surroundings. Ghosts haunted this space. Not in a literal sense — the ghosts here were only in his mind. His sister had drawn her last pain-filled breath within these walls, twelve years earlier.

In those days the books lining the shelves had been quite different, but the space was still a library. It was here where he first saw the entity that had set him on his current path. He'd received a glimpse of the abyss that day but instead of retreating, he chose to venture deeper.

A psychologist would've said Casca was trying to conquer his fears and atone for his inability to save his sister. A form of survivor's guilt, perhaps. By facing the darkness he might find a way to master it.

That's why he'd never moved and tried to put any distance between himself and his memories. The library served as a constant reminder of what lurked in the shadows. It had become his personal Ground Zero, focusing his obsession and giving shape to the mission ahead.

For twelve years Casca had studied every occult tradition known to man, delving into mysteries that should remain out of the reach of mere mortals. His wealth put him in a unique position, allowing him to indulge this obsession to a degree impossible for the average person.

But somewhere along the line Casca had reached an impasse. Studying the occult had ceased to be enough for him. What good was knowing the enemy if one never engaged him in battle? The years of silent contemplation were over. The time had arrived for direct action. A war was coming. Not a war where armies would clash on the battlefield. This would be a shadow war unfolding beneath the surface of normal society.

Casca was ready for the battle ahead. He had the will and the resources, but he was no soldier. At one point he'd contemplated using mercenaries. Financing a private army to battle this dark foe sounded good in theory, but less so in practice. Mercenaries would throw his money back at him once they knew what terrors they were up against. This wasn't a conflict that could be won by hired guns. He required someone who shared his dedication. Someone who understood that dark forces were gathering and needed to be stopped at all costs. Someone like Talon.

Casca had recognized the man's potential from the moment he first laid eyes on him. Talon was the knight he'd been searching for. The warrior who could take the fight to the enemy. They were both victims of the occult; they both brought their own specialized skills to the table. Together, they would be able to turn the tide in this conflict. Or so he hoped.

Now it appeared that he was losing the man. He blamed himself for pushing Talon away. He'd moved too fast. No one in their right minds would accept the dark truth without experiencing it firsthand.

Casca's eagerness had betrayed him and put the whole plan at risk. He prayed that the situation was reversible. Unfortunately, Talon's unwillingness to answer his calls didn't bode well. Either he had permanently turned his back or, worse, he was now in the hands of the enemy.

The latter possibility filled Casca with even greater dread. He needed the soldier to crush this cult.

Casca was yanked from his thoughts by his chirping cell. It was Jackson, one of his security men. "Mr. Casca, Talon has returned."

Casca's face flooded with relief. The incident at the Apple Store must have brought Talon back to his senses. Maybe he finally recognized that together, they stood a far better chance of defeating Zagan.

"Send him in."

The phone went dead.

Casca navigated the maze of shelves and occult objects until he reached the library's main chamber. Jackson and Talon grew visible in the near distance.

"Talon, it's good to see you..." The words trailed off as the Delta operator's hand came up in one smooth motion, Glock leveled. A stunned Jackson went for his gun but Talon viciously pistol-whipped him. The guard lost his balance and slammed into one of the occult display cases in an explosion of glass.

Talon sighted down on Casca and unleashed a fusillade of lead. Bullets strafed the air and perforated a row of books. The mysterious tomes erupted in clouds of paper and shredded binding. Talon emptied the magazine as Casca retreated into the aisles of the library.

Zagan must've somehow gotten to Talon. Casca had speculated that the cultists were under some form of supernatural control. Talon's conversion suggested that this was indeed the case.

What could he do? Casca didn't stand a chance against a super-soldier like Talon. He kept a gun in his desk drawer, but he doubted that he'd get the opportunity to draw it without being struck down first.

He had to find a way to reach Talon. To break the spell he was under. If he could make it back to his office, there might be a way. This mad gamble was his best shot at saving both Talon and himself.

More bullets lashed the air. Two more display cases exploded.

Casca scrambled into his office, heart pounding as Talon gained behind him. He surged toward his laptop, the screen still flickering with occult code. He reached the computer just as Talon stepped into the office, gun up.

Casca regarded the Delta operator. Some force had drained all the humanity from Talon's eyes and filled the void with lethal intent.

"Talon, this isn't who you are! Zagan murdered Michelle! You must fight this…"

For a moment, the gun wavered in Talon's hand, but the hesitation didn't extinguish the fearsome darkness in his slitted gaze.

Talon brought up his gun.

Casca punched the laptop's play button, streaming the terrible footage he'd discovered on its hard drive earlier that day to the 90-inch plasma TV-screen in his office.

As the big-screen TV ignited to life with the laptop's video images, Talon pulled the trigger.

***

Talon's world had become a place of darkness. A world where all his thoughts were drowned out by the occult program. For a split second, though, Casca's words almost seemed to make sense. What was his target talking about? Who was Michelle? In the far recesses of his mind, a memory stirred but was quickly suppressed. He served Zagan. He served the darkness. The billionaire's words were meant to confuse him. Distract him from his true purpose. They were nothing but a pack of lies. Weak attempts at throwing him off.

He raised the Glock. His fingers whitened on the trigger. And that's when a familiar face splashed on the monitor.

Why did he recognize this woman? There was something familiar about her. Hooded attackers wearing silver robot masks surrounded her. A quiver ran up his arm as he fired. His aim was off and the bullet missed Casca, shattering the illuminated globe instead. The bullet punched a giant hole into the Atlantic and the globe's light extinguished.

The images on the plasma screen were affecting him somehow. Doubt coiled up inside him. This time it took root and began to spread.

Talon stared at the scene playing out on the display. His breath hitched as the first knife plunged into the hapless female. The shakes traveled up his arm until his whole body was trembling. Was that a tear forming in his eye? It couldn't be.

His mind reeled and recoiled. Confusion and darkness gave way to dawning understanding. He remembered how he knew this woman... her voice was so familiar...

Michelle.

The name wormed its way through his consciousness, an echo of another life.

My Michelle...

She was in danger. The men onscreen were hurting her. Killing her.

They killed her!

Understanding shattered the darkness inside him and clarity returned with each successive thrust of the knife. As Michelle's life ran out onscreen, Talon dropped the gun. The Glock hit the carpet with a thump that reverberated all the way into his soul. Casca's voice sliced into his awareness.

"Talon, these monsters killed your Michelle."

No!

"They're using you."

This can't be.

"Are you going to let them get away with murder?"

NOOOOOOO!

A pitiful scream of unbridled anguish welled up and broke free from the depths of his darkest pain. Seeing Michelle die again shattered his defenses, stripped him of his emotional armor, tore through skin, muscle, sinew and bone straight to the core of his being.

Talon collapsed to the ground, sobbing. The video ended. Silence descended over Casca's office.

The man who lowered his head had been

Zagan's servant. The man who stared up at Casca was the occult assassin. "Help me kill these bastards."

CHAPTER NINETEEN

WAVES OF AGONY rippled through Talon's scarred chest. The inverted pentagram throbbed, the anguish like a physical manifestation of his pulsing rage. Zagan had taken away everything that mattered. His friend. His lover. His soul. Thanks to Casca, the Omicron CEO had ultimately failed on the last count.

Talon stole a glance at the billionaire's security guy, Jackson. The man was massaging his bruised jaw. Talon had no memory of clocking him but was grateful he hadn't resorted to lethal force. Perhaps on a subconscious level he'd been exerting control during his own possession, reigning in the violence in some way. Nevertheless, if it hadn't been for Casca's quick thinking he would've succumbed to the power of the occult algorithm.

He would have taken life in the name of Zagan's cult.

The billionaire pointed at the laptop on his oak desk. It was running the code segment. Talon's instinct was to recoil from the shimmering data, but Casca had reassured him it was safe. This was a small part of the program that couldn't exert any supernatural influence over him.

"So run this by me again," Talon said. "How is this software allowing Zagan to control reality?"

"The program is tapping into occult energy. It might help to think of it as a 21st Century version of a spell. The incantations embedded in the computer code are written in *demotic,* an ancient Egyptian language used in rituals to raise demons from the netherworld."

"The netherworld? You mean like hell?"

"In a manner of speaking. Mind you, we're not talking about Satan or the Judeo-Christian hell here."

"So what are we talking about?" Talon was doing his best to reign in his impatience. He wasn't used to not being in control.

"The darkness."

Talon cocked an eyebrow.

"I don't know if there's one absolute truth in this world," Casca explained. "What I do know is there's good and evil. Two cosmic forces coursing through our universe, in constant conflict. The light and the dark. All cultures have interpreted these forces in various way. Their poets dreamt up names, their artists gave it form, their priests designed rituals. The demons and monsters and mythologies of the popular imagination are man's attempt to grasp the darkness, a power beyond our knowledge and understanding."

The old Talon would've groaned at this point, but his recent experiences had changed his attitude. All this occult stuff was still giving him a headache but he couldn't deny the nightmare he'd lived through.

"So this *darkness* or demon is taking over Zagan?" Talon asked.

"Based on what you're describing, it appears that way. Zagan has become the vessel for a supernatural entity's return to the material world."

"Why does an ancient demon return as a cyborg?"

"The demon doesn't choose his form, the adept does. Its final manifestation is filtered through Zagan's mind and psychology. His dreams, his nightmares."

"Why does Zagan want to be possessed by this entity?"

"Oh, he doesn't."

Talon knitted his brows. Casca was losing him.

"Zagan believes he's controlling the darkness, when in fact it's controlling him. It's given him a taste of power so he'll finish the program."

"In other words, he's being played."

"Exactly. The darkness needs Zagan and his followers to fall. One final sacrifice is needed to complete the program and assure the demon's manifestation in our reality."

"Are you saying what I think you're saying? Omicron is headed for a Jim Jones-style mass suicide?"

Casca nodded gravely. "The Apple attack proves that Zagan is losing his sense of self-preservation. It's only a matter of time before the authorities put it all together and come after him. A final showdown approaches."

"And once this final sacrifice completes the program..."

"The demon will permanently enter our world. And it gets worse."

Talon groaned. "You gotta be kidding me."

"Becky managed to identify the code segment. It's part of Omicron's new operating system. Scheduled to automatically update at noon today, on all their devices."

"What does that mean?"

"This program is designed to raise demons from the darkness. Occult ritual updated for a new millennium and transformed into a computer program. Once it's out there, it can be replicated indefinitely. Anyone who comes in contact with the code will be able to raise and channel these entities, just as Zagan did. The program will be impossible to destroy, unless you track down each and every device and destroy them all."

Talon cracked his knuckles and a bead of cold sweat pulsed down his face. Casca's message was coming through loud and clear. If Zagan's program went live, it could mean the end. For everyone.

"Let's get to the fun part. How do we destroy this fucking program?"

"We hit the Omicron servers."

Talon pondered this for a moment. "Which means I gotta go back in there."

"It's the only way to end this thing."

Talon pointed at his brutalized chest. "I'm one of them now. Should make it easy to get past security. But what if Zagan pulls off another magic show?"

"I might be able to help you out on that front." Casca removed a circular pendant from his drawer. Inside the circle was a five-pointed star.

"I think I got my own," Talon said.

"This one is a little different," Casca said with a smile. "People see the pentagram as a representation of evil, but nothing could be farther from the truth. The five points represent the five senses, the five wounds of Christ, the five virtues of knighthood..."

"I get it. The pentagram can be a symbol of good. So how does it get such a bad rap?"

"In the 19th Century the interpretation changed," Casca explained. "With a single point facing upwards it was considered good, the spirit ruling over the element of matter."

Casca turned the pentacle upside down and now it resembled Talon's scar. "A reversed pentagram, with its two point upwards, became a symbol of evil because it overturns the proper order of things, putting matter above the spirit."

"So what am I supposed to do with it?"

"The pendant dates back to the Sumerian period. It represents a powerful force of good. Wear it when you face Zagan and his power over your senses will diminish."

Talon touched the pentagram amulet, not quite convinced. The metal was cool to the touch. No magical electricity here. Nevertheless, he pocketed the item. He would need all the help he could get.

"Anything else?"

"Let me show you something." Casca rose from behind his desk and walked back into the library. Talon trailed him. The place didn't seem all that eerie any more. Compared to some of the shit Talon had experienced back at Omicron, Casca's library was downright cozy.

"By the way, sorry for being a dick earlier," said Talon. "You were trying to warn me, but I wouldn't listen."

"I must apologize too. My over-eagerness got the best of me. You weren't ready for the truth."

"I am now." There was determination in Talon's voice.

Casca stepped up to one of the display cases. Talon leaned closer. Contained inside the glass case was a dagger inscribed with strange occult symbols.

"Do you like horror films?"

"You mean when I'm not living in one? To be honest I prefer comedies."

"No accounting for taste, eh?" Casca grinned. "I assume you're not familiar with the seven blades of Megiddo, from the *Omen* series of films?"

Talon shook his head. "You assume correctly."

"In the movies, seven sacred blades were created in Megiddo, the birthplace of Christianity, from the material of a comet. These magic blades were designed to kill Satan's progeny. The Antichrist."

"Lovely. Don't tell me this is one of these blades."

"Oh no, the blades are made up. Pulled from

the imagination of some Hollywood screenwriter. But the idea was inspired by this particular item..." Casca pointed at the knife in the case. "The demon slayer."

Talon eyed the knife more closely. The craftsmanship was impeccable. Its polished steel glittered in the library's recessed lights. Symbols were inscribed on the blade and the handle was fashioned from the bone of some animal.

"The demon slayer goes as far back as Babylonian times."

"How much did this toothpick set you back?"

"Let's say it made for a nice tax write-off, and leave it at that."

"Does it work?" Talon asked.

"It works."

Talon studied Casca, but the billionaire didn't add anything else. Talon sensed that there was a story here but it wouldn't be told today.

Casca opened the display case and handed Talon the knife. *Demon Slayer.* The weight of the ancient blade felt weird at first but seemed to adjust to his hand and grip, almost as if it was becoming an extension of his being.

He slashed the air a few times, testing how it felt in his hand. Could eight inches of pre-Christian steel stop a monster like Zagan? Talon wasn't quite convinced. But he had come to trust Casca.

"Between the demon slayer and the amulet you have a fighting chance at stopping Zagan."

"That's all I'm asking for."

Talon was about to get his rematch with Zagan.

This time around, only one of them would be left standing.

CHAPTER TWENTY

TALON STRODE INTO the Omicron lobby around eleven o'clock. The demon-slayer blade was securely sheathed under his jeans, amulet stashed in the pocket of his worn leather jacket.

Talon fixed his attention on the guards fronting the reception desk. Two of the men were approaching fast, expressions serious and focused.

Instead of presenting a security badge he opened his jacket, revealing the dried, crusted blood of the pentagram scar. His express ticket to hell.

The guards relaxed. These weren't polished GQ types, as he had first thought from a distance. They had cleaned up pretty well, but there was a toughness and an edge to these men. Former bikers or vets. Rough types with hard faces, ropy muscles and cold eyes. The suits and ties couldn't hide all their tats and scars.

Was the security staff under the spell of the occult algorithm, or true believers of the darkness? Talon wasn't a gambling man, but he'd bet on the second explanation with them.

One glance at his pentagram and the guards

backed off.

"I'm here to see my master," Talon said, doing his best to stay in character without overplaying his hand. One of the guards sidled up to him and indicated that Talon should follow him. He fell in step with the guard as they headed toward a bank of elevators.

Thanks to his last, rather memorable visit, the glass palace had lost much of its luster. He'd seen the true face of Omicron — the evil that lurked behind the polished surface.

Becky had informed them that Omicron's server maze was located on the lower level. Access was granted to the top coders and security staff. The guard walking Talon to the elevators was his way in.

As soon as they stepped into the lift and the door zoomed shut, Talon grabbed the man's neck and smashed his head against the elevator's control panel — full force. Ignoring the cams, he pulled the slumping guard's head back by his hair and pressed the demon-slayer blade against his carotid artery. Talon didn't know if the knife actually possessed the power to slay monsters, but it sure as hell would have no trouble opening up a man's throat.

"Slight change in plans. Last time I asked for the tour, they skipped the basement."

"Fuck you…" The guard's words were cut off as his forehead connected with the elevator wall again. Talon tore the security badge from the guard's breast-pocket and inserted it into a slot. A panel slid open, revealing a biometric touch screen.

He pushed the groggy guard in front of the screen. A beam of light zipped over the monitor, scanning the guard's eyeball. A second later, a touch-screen flashed into view. Talon selected the basement and the elevator hummed to life.

"Your friend begged for his life, ya' know," the guard mumbled under his breath.

Talon grew still as he tilted his head at this. Blood trickled down the guard's broken nose as his mouth creased into a dirty smile. "He squealed like a pig—"

The words died on his lips as Talon drove the blade through his ribcage, straight into his heart. The guard spat at him with his dying breath before staggering away.

A red circle was widening where the knife had entered. He slid down the wall, trailing a smear of blood, and crumpled on the elevator floor in a widening pool of gore.

Fuck! Talon cursed himself. He'd originally planned to keep the guard alive, at least until he was inside the server farm. Studying the dead guard, Talon did recognize him as one of Erik's killers. Wherever Erik might be, Talon knew he was grinning like a schoolboy.

This one's for you, old friend.

The elevator stopped and the doors parted. Talon stepped into a narrow hallway and navigated through another doorway that required the guard's security badge.

Two IT engineers faced a bank of monitors inside the a glass-enclosed control deck overlooking an endless maze of servers. They gazed up at Talon with surprise. One of the IT guys reacted immediately and sprang to his feet, knife up. Talon grabbed a nearby coffee pot and hurled its boiling contents into the IT guy's face. The IT guy screamed and backed away.

The second engineer whipped out a blade, his binary tattoo exposed as he rushed Talon. The Delta operator stepped aside and yanked the engineer's arm back until it snapped. The knife went flying.

Three punches later and the engineer had joined his buddy on the ground.

A second door whirred open. Talon advanced into the server maze. A knight entering the lair of the dragon.

The server farm stretched out before him, a cold, sterile maze of pulsing technology. Talon's footsteps echoed eerily as he penetrated the otherworldly computer labyrinth. The marble black servers that dotted the white, cavernous space made Talon think of electronic coffins in a mausoleum. Glittering futuristic graves containing the remains of some computer race of the distant future.

Talon didn't know which of the black monoliths housed Zagan's demonic program, but it didn't matter. He would blow the whole basement sky-high. Moving with speed, all too aware that the clock was ticking, he set his C-4 charges and armed them. One after another, the lights on the explosives glimmered red while the remote detonator remained secure in his jacket pocket.

The plan was to set off the C-4 and get the hell

out of here. But if his enemy left him no choice, Talon was prepared to die in this basement. Whatever ancient entity Zagan had brought back to life couldn't be allowed to return to the 21st Century and multiply. The world had enough problems without having to worry about a demonic invasion.

Talon had set about eight charges when the hairs on his neck and arms stood up. Something had changed inside the server maze. He shivered and realized the temperature had dropped by ten degrees or more. He peered down the spooky, abandoned hallway. The computers shined with an unnatural life and the ventilation system hummed forebodingly.

He was about to shift his attention back to the task at hand when reality tilted once more. Something unnatural was unfolding at the end of the server passageway. For a second the air rippled and thin tendrils of condensation snaked around the monolithic computers. A fog was forming, and spreading rapidly.

The old Talon would have stared with incomprehension at the surreal spectacle. The new Talon had been waiting for Zagan to make his move.

Talon's fingers closed around the pentacle and draped it over his neck.

"This had better work."

Ahead of him, the ghostly fog swirled and parted, revealing a new arrival on the scene.

Zagan.

CHAPTER TWENTY-ONE

SERRONE ENTERED THE police morgue, her head pounding. She'd snacked on Ibuprofen for breakfast and washed the pills down with about a gallon of coffee, but still she was running on fumes.

Her stomach lurched as she eyed the bodies laid out on a series of slabs. A morgue attendant and three pathologists worked the tables, engaged in the thankless task of separating the cultists from the massacre victims. The killers were civilians too. All races, ages and religions were represented and connected by one identifying mark — the binary tattoo etched on their forearms.

A clear pattern was emerging among the attackers. The majority of cultists worked at Omicron. This couldn't be a coincidence. There had to be a link to the tech company.

Making things worse, the whole case had gone nuclear. It was world news now and only a matter of time before the FBI and Homeland Security joined the party. Serrone was almost hoping they'd pull her off the investigation and assign some hotshot Fed to head the case. What she'd seen at the Apple Store wasn't like anything she'd ever experienced or wanted to experience again. At least her partner, Grell, was now in stable condition.

While the brass figured out what the next official move should be, Serrone was going to check out their sole true lead. Omicron. She was going to visit the company's headquarters in Silicon Valley and begin asking the hard questions.

With any luck, those questions would make the right people uncomfortable and someone would start talking. No way all these employees belonged to a cult without someone else at the company being aware of the situation.

She nodded at Detective Dawson to join her. The man was in his early forties, a good cop but a bit too by-the-book for Serrone's taste. A close friend of Grell's, he was itching to get to the bottom of these murders. That made him a perfect ally.

As they drove to Omicron, Serrone called her house and managed to get her daughter on the phone. Seven-year-old Casey was getting ready for school. Serrone's mother had been nice enough to watch Casey last night when it became clear she would be pulling overtime.

"Hi Mom, is everything okay?"

It was great to hear her daughter's voice. The kid seemed to have the wisdom of someone five times her age. "Honey, mommy is fine. I just need to wrap up something at work. By the time you're home from school I'll be back, I promise. We'll grab dinner tonight, your pick."

Casey paused on the other end, almost as if she doubted the veracity of her mother's words. It broke

Serrone's heart. Sometimes she hated being a cop.

As she hung up the phone, Serrone fought back a wave of anxiety. How could she do this to her daughter? The poor kid had already lost her dad. Why did she have to be cursed with a mother who carried a gun to work?

She bit her lip and took another sip of coffee, welcoming the bitter taste on her tongue. She eyed the officers in the car and realized that she missed Grell's entertaining banter. He could be an opinionated ass, but he made her laugh. They were a good team.

Unfortunately, despite his good intentions Dawson was blessed with the personality of a valium.

About forty minutes later, they pulled up to Omicron and got out of the vehicle. Sunlight sparkled on the company's logo, above the main entrance. Plenty of people in Serrone's circle swore by Omicron's technology. *Omicron is even better than Apple!* Whatever. In her mind Omicron was just another Silicon Valley tech conglomerate making stuff that encouraged people to stare at their devices instead of paying attention to each other.

After some back and forth with Omicron's overeager security staff, they were finally escorted to the offices of Travis Hockney, Senior Vice President of Public Relations. Serrone planned to ask him if the leadership at Omicron was aware of a cult recruiting their workers? Had Hockney seen any employees sporting the binary tattoo?

As they crossed the vast atrium of the high-tech

palace, Serrone marveled at the building's breathtaking architectural design. The bright and airy environment struck her as the ideal workplace, a far cry from her cramped gray quarters at the police department.

They walked through an entertainment room where workers depressurized. There were foosball and Ping-Pong tables alongside arcade games from the 1980s. Another doorway led to a large office space lined with cubicles.

A young, attractive woman stepped up to them. "Hello Detective, my name is Stacy and I'm Hockney's assistant. He's taking a call but will be right with you. Would you care for a water or juice while you wait?"

Serrone asked for an energy drink instead. Today wasn't the day to quit bad habits. As they waited, she studied the workspace more closely. Hockney's office was a separate room at the far end of a much larger work area. Men and women, most of them in their twenties and thirties, faced their computer stations. The desks were decorated with toys and other examples of geek culture. Serrone saw a Star Wars screensaver and action figures from some comic-book flick.

These Nerf-ball warriors didn't strike her as vicious killers, but she'd felt the same way about the attackers back in the Apple Store.

As Serrone sorted through these impressions, all activity in the office suddenly ceased. No typing, no phone calls, no conversation. Everyone sat ramrod straight in their Aeron chairs, eyes fixed on their screens.

Curious, Serrone took a step closer. To her surprise, all the monitors showed the same strange stream of data. She leaned forward, hoping to get a reaction from one of the workers — perhaps a hello or some form of acknowledgement — but the Omicron tech-heads remained in their drone-like trance state.

Serrone was getting a bad feeling about this place, once again reminded of the blank fanaticism she'd encountered during the attack on the Apple Store. She chewed her lip and balled the keychain in her pocket until her hand hurt.

"This is ridiculous," she said to Dawson, who projected a calm rivaling the monk-like Omicron workers. "How long are they going to keep us waiting?"

Dawson shrugged in response. Serrone shook her head and scoped the office floor for Hockney's assistant. The young woman seemed to have vanished into thin air.

Fed up, Serrone pivoted and strode briskly toward Hockney's office. She knocked on the closed door. No one answered. She repeated her knocking. Still no response.

Impatience boiling over, she pushed into Hockney's office to find him slumped back in his chair, shirt soaked with blood, a wide gash in his throat.

Jesus...

Serrone went for her pistol. Weapon out, she circled the desk and glimpsed Hockney's assistant hemorrhaging red on the hardwood floor. Her legs twitched, heels bobbing up and down. Hockney must've assaulted her first before killing himself.

Next to his lifeless features, the same strange computer code slashed over his monitor. Serrone's blood turned to ice. The horror she'd first experienced in the Apple Store had followed her to Omicron.

CHAPTER TWENTY-TWO

TALON AND ZAGAN faced other in the server maze, about a hundred feet between them. Two classic adversaries gearing up for the bitter, final confrontation. Zagan's physical condition was worsening at a geometric rate. The skin was stretched taut against his skull and pockmarked by a shimmering patchwork of circuitry. Steel fingers pierced through a fraying layer of broken skin and made his hands look like bloody gloves worn by a robot.

Advancing down the corridor of servers, the flickering lights on the explosive charges extinguished one by one as soon as Zagan passed them. His mere presence was manipulating the material world.

Talon's heart sank.

"I don't know how you broke free of my program, Sergeant, but you're too late."

We'll see about that, Talon thought.

The fog thickened and the temperature dropped a few degrees. Casca had said the pendant would protect him from Zagan's reality hacks, but so far it was doing jack shit.

Talon's hand came up with the Glock in it and he started firing into the demonic cyborg-creature closing in on him. Bullets might be useless against his enemy, but Talon didn't want Zagan to catch on that he might have an ace up his sleeve. Lead slammed into Zagan in hot spurts, each round connecting with its target in a fiery eruption of flesh and steel. The bullets stitched bloody patterns on his chest. It barely slowed down the monster's inexorable approach.

Talon replaced the magazine in his weapon with a metallic snap. For Talon to use the *Demon Slayer*, Zagan needed to move in closer. As long as Zagan felt secure in his superiority, it would be easier to lure him into a close-combat situation. Talon prayed that Casca's fearsome knife would prove more effective than his talisman had.

His thoughts were interrupted when the roiling carpet of frosty mist engulfed him, erasing Zagan from view. The freezing fog swallowed the blinking servers, too. He tried to focus on his other senses. Were those incoming footfalls?

Talon squinted, desperately hoping to penetrate the thick fog. He sensed more than saw vague movement, but it was too late. A fist popped out of the mist and found him. With the force of a brick slamming into the side of his face, Zagan's inhuman punch hurtled him through the air.

Talon crashed into one of the blinking servers. The sharp impact rattled his bones. *Fuck...* He never saw the attack coming. Zagan had struck seemingly out of nowhere. At this rate, the fight would be over before it started.

Zagan was closing in fast. Another attack was surely just a second away. Talon whirled as Zagan's metallic foot shot out at him from the icy fog. It hit the space where his head had been an instant earlier and pulverized the server in a shower of sparking electronics.

How did one fight an invisible, superhuman enemy? Talon's surroundings swarmed with shadows. His senses struggled to penetrate the layered gloom. The mist rippled and Zagan's skull-face thrust toward him with ferocious speed. The head-butt sent Talon reeling backwards a couple of feet.

Crimson sheeted down his face and the taste of iron coated his mouth. He spit blood and realized one more attack like the last one and he'd be done for.

He needed to fight back. Somehow. But merely grazing Zagan with the *Demon Slayer* would alert his adversary of the magical weapon in his arsenal. He'd have to play his cards right and strike only when he spotted a real opportunity to do some damage.

Talon needed to buy himself some time... Get Zagan to reveal his position in the living fog. Talon thought he'd gotten to Zagan the other day. The right words might trigger a similar intense psychological response.

"You're being played like a chump."

No answer.

"You think you're controlling this power, Zagan,

but take a quick look in the mirror and you'll see who is in the driver's seat."

"What are you talking about?"

At least a reaction. *Good.*

"The darkness is destroying you."

"The darkness serves me," Zagan hissed, rage pulsing. "It's making me stronger." Each word sounded like it was being torn from Zagan's throat, the transformation distorting his voice.

"You're fooling yourself. This entity is killing you. You're dying."

Air whistled and Talon jumped aside. The disrupted fog swirled and Zagan smashed into another server.

Okay, finally we're getting somewhere...

As this hopeful thought cut through his mind, the amulet around his neck suddenly lit up. The wave of occult energy warmed his flesh, but there was no pain. Electricity burst from the pendant and rippled through his body. An instant later, the fog parted and there stood Zagan, mere inches from Talon's face, gearing up for his next attack.

Damn, it does work!

Zagan's iron fist blasted at him and Talon sidestepped the deadly blow with trained grace, drawing the *Demon Slayer* in mid-movement. The knife came up and scythed across Zagan's throat from left to right. For a stunned beat, the Omicron CEO stood there. Then he took two weak steps back and his second mouth spouted blood. It splattered the steel servers and pearled on the pristine white floor. Disbelief flickered across Zagan's features.

How could the blade harm him when bullets had failed?

Talon assumed a close-quarters fighting stance, but it was too late. Zagan had regained his bearings. His arm lanced out with pneumatic force. Fingers powered by superhuman strength snapped around Talon's wrist, squeezing until the viselike grip forced him to drop the *Demon Slayer*. Zagan kicked the knife aside and with devastating force rammed Talon into one of the servers.

What happened next turned even Talon's battle-hardened stomach. Zagan's fingers dug under the flaps of skin lining his gushing throat and pulled off his face in one violent motion. It felt like a mask coming off, the shocking act exposing glistening bone and shiny musculature interspersed with dull steel and glittering cybernetics. A steel skull sheathed in slick gore and patches of oozing tissue glared back at Talon. The wet eyes boring into him were still organic. A demonic fusion of man and machine had taken place.

Zagan was wounded but a long way from being defeated. Talon had to get his hands on the *Demon Slayer,* which now rested about ten feet from where he stood.

Talon scrambled past the servers, heading for the knife. He never made it.

Zagan bolted forward and closed the gap between them before Talon could reach the supernatural weapon. Lightning fast, Zagan's arm flashed and he seized Talon's throat. Feet dangling above the floor, the Delta operator desperately choked for air. The bones of his neck cracked. A few ounces of pressure and it would all be over.

He only dimly made out Zagan's next chilling words. "I pledge your soul to my master."

***

Serrone burst out of Hockney's office, one hand clutching her gun and the other nervously palming her phone. She was calling for backup but so far failing to get through. How was she not getting a signal in one of the most wired places on the fucking planet?

Dawson stared at her wide-eyed. "What's going on?"

"Phone's dead and something is messing up the Wi-Fi, if you can believe that. We better get the hell out of here and call for backup. Hockney and his assistant are dead."

"Oh shit." Dawson craned his neck to catch a view of Hockney's office and shuddered at the sight.

Nice to see that the man has a pulse, Serrone thought crazily.

"Let's go." She grabbed Dawson's arm and pulled him into motion. Dawson fell in step with her, both glad to be leaving the eerie cubicle area behind.

All the engineers remained frozen in tableau as they surged past them, hypnotized by their machines and oblivious to the officers' presence. How long before they snapped out of their unnatural trance and turned into a murderous mob? Serrone couldn't explain it logically but she sensed that the program must be the source of this madness. Somehow it was exerting a terrible pull on these people.

Guard up, Serrone and Dawson crossed the vast atrium. The previously idyllic setting was now filled with hidden horrors and dark potential. What other dangers lurked behind the cheerful facade?

They had almost reached the front security desk when a strange whistling sound cut through the air, followed by a thump. Serrone whirled. A body lay sprawled on the lobby floor in a broken, bloody mass, face planted in the floor and features caved in. At first Serrone didn't quite grasp what she was staring at. How had this person died? She trailed Dawson's gaze as he tilted his head up at the upper floors.

Omicron workers loomed on the second and third-floor catwalks. They were in the process of climbing over the glass railings. A frightful realization hit Serrone. The pulped worker beside her was a jumper and these other tech professionals were about to join the first suicide.

No... Don't do it...

Serrone mouthed the word "no" but her trembling lips produced no sound. She averted her gaze as two more cultists hit the hard lobby floor with a wet splat and the sickening crunch of bones breaking.

Oh my God...

She spun toward the security guys. They'd all

drawn their guns. One man fired, hitting Dawson before pointing the pistol at his own temple and pulling the trigger. He went down in a spray of red, his brain savagely splattering the terminals of the security desk. Two more pops followed in quick succession as the other two guards blew their brains out and collapsed.

Terror flared in Serrone. She wished with all her heart that she'd never come to Omicron today. Wished she was at home, feeling the warmth of her daughter's cheek against her own and tousling Casey's soft hair instead of clutching the cold grip of her pistol.

She struggled to suppress her mounting panic. One look at poor Dawson told her that any help would come too late. She was still rooted in place when approaching footfalls rattled the blood-clotted lobby. Three engineers were zeroing in on her with quick, determined strides. They all wielded blades in their outstretched hands and were closing in fast. Even more disturbing, the incoming horde was cutting off the main entrance, her one way out of this madhouse.

Serrone fired away and the three cultists spun around in an explosion of brains and blood. Their bodies were still twitching as six new cultists took their place. Serrone knew she was doomed. She wouldn't be able to hit every one of her pursuers before they reached her. The unstoppable throng surged forward and she started running.

They were herding her toward the assembly hall located at the other end of the lobby. No choice but to play along. She kicked open the wooden door and powered into the auditorium, determined to blow away anyone lurking in the shadows. To her relief, the narrow aisle leading into the assembly hall was deserted.

She slammed the door shut and moved deeper into the vast space. She soon recognized that she wasn't alone in the cavernous chamber. An audience of engineers hammered away on their laptops while images of the progressing mass suicide filled the screens before them.

A snapping sound behind her made her spin away from the screen. A programmer had closed his laptop lid. The scene repeated itself as other engineers sealed their computers and rose to their feet, their empty eyes fixating on her now. She held up her pistol even though she knew this crowd wouldn't be intimidated by the weapon. These men and women were beyond reason. Beyond any instinct for self-preservation. These were slaves to a digital master she couldn't comprehend. She was up against a seething mob of fanatics who all shared the same goal…

Murder.

CHAPTER TWENTY-THREE

TALON FELT HIS life draining away.

The tendons in his neck stood out like cords and his temple pulsed. Zagan's nightmarish robot skull-face dripped gore. The one weapon that could offer Talon a fighting chance remained tantalizingly out of his reach. He was about to succumb to the inhuman pressure on his windpipe when his darkening gaze landed on...

Michelle.

She had materialized about thirty feet behind Zagan. This wasn't the broken woman who'd perished in his blood-soaked arms. This Michelle was a vision to behold. She looked the way she did when he proposed to her in the park. Beautiful. Untouched by death. Full of life.

Sadness welled up inside him but he drew a strange comfort from the idea that they might be reunited soon. To his surprise, instead of welcoming the possibility of his passing, Michelle whispered one word that changed everything.

Live.

Talon's bloodshot gaze traveled back to Zagan. He took in the pulsing servers. Remembered the stakes. This wasn't about him or personal vengeance any longer. Three hundred Omicron workers were in danger of committing suicide. Who knew how many lives would be lost if this hellish program infiltrated the operating system of every Omicron device in the world?

Talon had dedicated his life to keeping his country safe. He'd sworn to protect America against all enemies, foreign and domestic. Zagan couldn't be allowed to win.

Tapping into the last of his dwindling reserves of strength, Talon reached for the pentacle around his neck and pushed it against Zagan's hand, hoping this desperate move might have some sort of effect.

As soon as the amulet made contact with Zagan, he roared with savage agony and let go of Talon. The Delta operator crashed to the floor and rolled away. He scanned his surroundings and locked on the *Demon Slayer*. Killer instinct flashed in his eyes as he scooped up the magical knife. Tapping into his rage, he honed his fury until its razor edge rivaled the blade in his hand. This was for everyone Zagan had sacrificed in his mad quest for power.

For Erik.

For Michelle.

His hand tightened around the blade and spun, steel slicing in a lethal arc. He slashed Zagan's chest, once, twice before driving the weapon deep into the cyborg-demon's heart. The *Demon Slayer* penetrated metal, circuitry and tissue to find the abomination's pulsating heart.

Zagan bellowed and the server room shook with

his roars of pain. He stumbled back and clutched the hilt of the blade sticking from his chest. Before he could liberate it from his flesh, Talon's leg flashed out in a roundhouse kick that drove the handle of the knife even deeper into Zagan's ribcage.

A second later, the charges ignited back to life and the ticking countdown resumed. Weakened by the attack, Zagan's power over reality was growing more tenuous.

Two minutes left before the explosives would go off - two minutes for Talon to get the hell out of here.

Talon spun around and dashed toward the control deck. As he sprinted down the passage of pulsating servers, he searched for Michelle but saw no sign of his love. Had a trick of his imagination conjured her into existence? Or had Michelle somehow communicated from the beyond? Talon didn't have the answer. All he knew was that her presence, imagined or not, had given him the necessary strength he needed to defeat Zagan.

Talon reached the elevator and punched the call button. Sensing movement behind him, he pivoted toward his pursuer. The biomechanical monster lurching toward him was barely human, a cyberpunk nightmare of fizzling robotics and bleeding meat.

Talon squeezed off round after round, pumping lead into the withering demon. The fusillade sent Zagan stumbling backward.

The elevator doors slammed shut just as the first

charge went off. Metal warped under the blast and Zagan's bestial shriek of defeat gave way to the deafening sound of an enormous explosion.

Shockwaves rattled the lift, but it continued its ascend. A beat later Talon reached the Omicron lobby and spilled into the atrium. Two steps farther from the destruction, the rest of Talon's explosives erupted in the basement below. The floor shook and trembled. Tile beneath his boots cracked and spiderwebbed. Shockwaves rippled through the structure and shattered windows. It rained glass.

And then it all stopped.

The lobby had been eviscerated and resembled a battlefield of fractured glass and broken humanity. Talon stumbled and staggered through the gutted atrium. He had almost reached the exit when he heard the familiar sound of a round being fired. The bullet would find him before he could even turn.

***

The horde was closing in. Circling and circling. They had become part of the occult program, a physical extension of the code.

Serrone squeezed off round after round but the shots echoed impotently in the auditorium. No one gave a shit about the gun in her hand. She was outnumbered and a few bullets shy from being out of ammunition.

She doubted that her predicament would be any different if she were facing a smaller group of fanatics. These people experienced no fear. They didn't care about their own survival. All that mattered to them was making a sacrifice to whatever unholy deity they worshipped. Her best option was to save the last bullet for herself but unlike the raging cultists, she had a reason to live. That reason was named Casey and she was seven years old and Serrone had promised to have dinner with her tonight. It couldn't end like this. She couldn't let Casey down. Not again.

Serrone was a tough woman but she could feel the hot tears welling up in her eyes. Going out like this just wasn't fair.

The mob was almost upon her when a loud explosion rocked the Omicron building, shaking the foundation of the structure. For a moment, the images on the large screen fritzed out, turning black, and she could hear glass pulverizing outside the auditorium.

Serrone was still trying to make sense of the sounds of destruction when the horde ceased its approach. They jerked up straight and slumped in unison as if a switch had been flipped. The cultists suddenly didn't look bloodthirsty anymore. Their faces wore expressions of shock, panicked eyes studying the knives in their hands. Stunned by their actions. Somehow the spell had been broken.

Taking in the change, Serrone allowed herself to experience an emotion she thought she'd never feel again: hope.

CHAPTER TWENTY-FOUR

FISHER COULDN'T BELIEVE what was happening. The explosion had solidified his growing dread. The servers had been breached. This disturbing insight was followed by another development. His fellow cultists were dropping their knives and returning to their senses. There was only one explanation...

Talon.

They'd been so close to completing the program. Rage flared inside Fisher and he swore he would find the man and teach him the true cost of his victory. Fisher would rebuild, gather a new flock. Omicron could not be stopped.

As these thoughts of vengeance consumed his mind and heart, footsteps echoed in the lobby below. He peered over the railing and saw Talon stumble from the elevators. Fisher's lip twisted into a cruel smile. *Payback's a bitch.*

He wished he could announce himself to his enemy, to make him suffer, but he expected Talon to be armed and wasn't taking any chances.

He sighted down on Talon.

Fired.

***

A muffled scream followed the explosive crack of the bullet. Talon whirled and saw Fisher spill from the first floor and crash to the lobby. The man's body jerked upon impact and grew still.

Who did he have to thank for saving his life?

Footfalls behind him. Talon turned. Staring back at him was Detective Serrone, gun leveled. Her hair was pasted to her forehead, features coated with perspiration and exhaustion. Who was he kidding — she probably cut a better figure than he did.

For a moment their eyes locked and Talon remained unsure of the detective's next move.

"What happened here today?" she asked.

Forgoing long-winded explanations, Talon said, "Evil was defeated."

His words seemed to satisfy Serrone. At least for now. The detective had saved his life. He would never forget her. Eying Serrone he said, "Thank you."

Talon turned away from the detective, her eyes convincing him that she wouldn't shoot him. She knew he was one of the good guys.

He staggered out of Omicron. Sirens keened in the distance as he stumbled to his motorcycle. He feared that in his battered state the cops might stop him, but he would have to chance it.

He swung onto the Ducati and shot out of the Omicron parking lot. He was long gone by the time the authorities arrived.

WILLIAM MASSA

CHAPTER TWENTY-FIVE

TALON DIDN'T REMEMBER how he got back to Casca's estate. He later was told that he collapsed from blood loss as soon as he parked his bike. For two straight days he slept, lost to the darkness that came with deep exhaustion.

Upon waking, he vaguely recalled some of his dreams. Michelle was in most of them. There was also a dim recollection of a doctor checking in on him, but perhaps he'd imagined the man. Reality and imagination had fused while his body was recovering.

The first change he noticed when he finally woke up was that someone – most likely the doctor in his dreams – had stitched up the wound on his chest. There would be a scar in the shape of the inverted star, no doubt about it. It would serve as a constant reminder of the evil he'd confronted and defeated in San Francisco.

There would be other enemies. As long as ruthless men could master the rituals of the occult, they would tap into its unspeakable power. Talon had received a glimpse into an alien world and come to realize that the universe was far grander

196

and more terrifying than he could've imagined.

After he showered and shaved, Casca brought him up to speed. Becky had returned to her life secure in the knowledge that this cult was history. The Omicron story still dominated the news channels. Experts left and right speculated about how this techno-cult could have gained such a hold over the minds of its followers. Deepening the mystery was the fact that many of the cultists suffered from a form of amnesia, or so they claimed.

Books would be written about the computer cult. Experts and pundits would be debating the case for weeks to come, at least until the next big disaster drowned out the chatter.

"Your two weeks are almost up, Sergeant," Casca said. "Time to report for duty soon."

Talon shook his head. "I won't be going back. At least not permanently."

Casca cocked an eyebrow.

"I'm resigning from Delta."

"Really?"

"There are plenty of good men fighting the war on terror. My services might be needed on another front."

"You think you're the guy who's going to save the world from the boogeyman?" Casca asked, echoing Talon's earlier question.

"Perhaps we can save it together," Talon replied.

They both grinned.

"Did we destroy the program?" Talon asked.

"I believe so."

"Where do we go from here?"

"I've been hearing some disturbing stories coming out of Milan. Someone is abducting tourists and leaving dead bodies behind... Bodies with pentagrams carved into their backs."

Talon winked. "I always wanted to visit Italy." His face grew serious as he continued. "I became a soldier to keep this country safe. My job hasn't changed. Only the enemy."

"Let's head inside and I'll show you the reports. See what you make of it."

Talon and Casca turned toward the estate.

They'd won a victory against the darkness, but the war was just beginning.

THE END

Mark Talon will return in Occult Assassin: Soul Jacker.

**PLEASE ENJOY A SPECIAL SAMPLE OF
OCCULT ASSASSIN: ICE SHADOWS**

CHAPTER ONE

WHIRLING SNOWFLAKES LANDED on Kristin's face like icy kisses as her athletic frame hurtled down the steep mountain at fifty-plus miles per hour. Sending sprays of powder into the air, she skied with the skill and carefree abandon of someone in their mid-twenties. All around her, a state-of-the art lighting system turned the tree-lined slopes into an azure, phantasmagorical winter wonderland.

Kristin had arrived in Bergen, Norway, less than 48 hours earlier. Originally from Oslo, she worked as an account executive for a large advertising firm in London but tried to visit as often as her hectic schedule permitted. After the failure of her most recent romantic relationship, a doomed coupling with a French commercial director, the mountains of her homeland had been calling her.

Ahead the trail forked and Kristin opted for the steeper, more challenging backcountry chute. Twilight deepened and the woods grew dark. With fewer light poles available, she'd have to rely on her other senses. She tightened her body, further increasing her speed.

For a moment her problems ceased to matter and she felt in complete control. How she wished some of that confidence extended to her love life. She had tried to convince herself that Pierre was just a fling, but she was heartbroken. Their relationship had lasted for less than a month before the flowers and fancy dinners gave way to unanswered calls and unreturned texts. After three days of radio silence, she'd gotten the hint – the Frenchman had moved on. Why had she thought she could tame a well-known Lothario and heartbreaker?

She was pulled out of her thoughts when her eyes landed on an unexpected obstacle directly ahead. A six-foot high wall of ice blocked the narrow trail. The blockade flexed and rippled in the starlight. She'd seen videos of ice heaves, tsunami-style waves of frozen water rippling over shorelines and damaging homes. She had forgotten the science behind the phenomenon, but she did know it occurred near lakes and required strong winds. So what had triggered such a strange anomaly at this high altitude? And why did it only seem to be affecting the ski trail?

All these thoughts slashed through her mind within a handful of seconds. The time for speculation had run out – the ice barrier was upon her. She had to act fast. A direct impact at this speed would kill her.

Kristin dug the edges of her skis into the powder. The maneuver sent her flying. Airborne, she twisted her body in midair and landed butt-first, as she'd been trained to do. Her derriere absorbed the brunt of the fall as she slid down the trail on her back. The powdery snow cushioned the impact and Kristin counted her blessings. An icy surface would have been far less pleasant.

For a moment she just lay there, the cold seeping through her ski jacket. Her breath misted in the chilly darkness. She predicted some ugly bruises in the morning, but her training and quick reflexes had spared her any broken bones. With a determined grunt Kristin performed a press up while holding the base of her poles with an uphill hand. Her upper body strength was well developed from regular gym visits and she quickly got back on her feet.

She dusted thick clumps of snow off her ski-suit and bindings before taking a closer look at the surreal sight in front of her. A row of frozen stalagmites jabbed into the air like the teeth of some buried ice giant.

Kristin shivered as she gained a stronger sense of her situation. She was alone on the deserted chute and no sound broke the unnerving silence. Making matters worse, one of the nearby light poles began to flicker and grow dark.

Shit! Other lights followed suit and winked off, drenching the mountain in darkness. The sole illumination now emanated from the dim stars overhead. What was going on? She decided to round the barrier and continue down the mountain as quickly as possible. She instinctively sensed that she was in danger.

To suppress her fear, she concentrated on the task at hand. She trudged along the frozen barricade, moving toward the tree-line on the left side of the trail. How she wished some other skier would materialize, but the odds were slim considering the late hour.

The sound of her skis crunching over the snow echoed eerily on the forlorn trail and her pulse quickened. The wind had picked up and now cut through her clothes. Her teeth chattered and each breath was like inhaling ice. So much for being inured to the cold. She always teased her British colleagues when they complained about their comparatively mild winters. But this was different. The temperature must have dropped over twenty degrees since she took her tumble in the snow. How was this possible?

She reached the trees and began to round the strange ice wall. Behind her the branches stirred, wooden fingers brushing against her back. She stifled a scream.

Get a grip on yourself!

Just a few more seconds and she'd be on her way, blasting down the trail and headed for the safety of the base about 800 feet below.

She suddenly noticed strange carvings etched into the trees. Her eyes narrowed and she had to lean forward to catch a better look. As a native Norwegian, she recognized the symbols as runes, the characters of the alphabet used by the ancient people of Northern Europe. She didn't know the meaning of these symbols, but it deepened her sense of dread. Heart hammering in her chest, she turned away from the trees and wove around the icy obstacle. Fear fueled her movements. Reality had narrowed to one simple objective — she had to get back on the trail.

Her singular focus paid off and she reached the other side of the ice wall, only to grow dead still... Three human silhouettes blocked the trail ahead.

A scream wanted to escape from Kristin's throat, but her lips were frozen shut. The tall, gaunt snowboarders loomed before her, creating a human barrier across the width of the chute. Even if she managed to somehow weave around them, nothing would stop them from chasing after her.

The spooky trio advanced. As they stepped into the moonlight, Kristin realized they all wore fiberglass skull-helmets favored by both hardcore snowboarders and paintballers. They looked more like monstrous, medieval skeleton creatures than masked humans.

Despite the punishing cold and her mounting terror, Kristin exploded into motion. Using her poles, she pushed away from the figures and shot back toward the trees.

She had barely advanced a few feet when a massive silhouette peeled from the shadow-soaked woods, barring her escape. Like the others, he wore a skull-mask that erased all humanity from his visage and a glittering knife extended from his gloved hand.

Kristin's piercing scream cut through the forest but was quickly drowned out by the unforgiving wind.

Chapter Two

THEY CALLED HIM the vampire.

His real name was Rezok and he was the lead singer of the Norwegian black metal band Ice God. He also happened to be the reason why Mark Talon, the occult assassin, had come to Bergen, Norway and found himself in a rundown pub surrounded by a mob of screaming, drunk fans. Any minute now Ice God would hit the stage, and the anticipation in the crowd was palpable.

Talon shared their excitement, but for different reasons. This was a recon mission and he hoped to catch a closer look at the enemy.

All eyes in the club remained riveted on the dark stage, lips mouthing the lyrics to their favorite doom-and-gloom songs. The surging throng wore exclusively black - any other color was frowned upon. Interspersed with the hardcore constituents were a few conservative-looking guys seeking to get drunk while listening to some gnarly Norwegian metal. Judging from the disapproving stares these outsiders received, the "real" fans considered them impersonators who lacked the balls to commit. It took more to make you a true member of the scene than loosening that tie and trading a pair of slacks for black jeans, after putting in a long week as a cubicle drone.

Talon's years as a special operator in Afghanistan and Iraq had taught him the value of blending in and becoming part of the scenery. He'd opted for the black metal uniform of choice: a leather jacket, jeans and steel-tipped combat boots. The T-shirt of an obscure Danish band with an illegible name sold the look. No one questioned the authenticity of his commitment to the movement. Or if they did, his six-foot-one, well-muscled frame and the fire in his eyes made them keep it to themselves.

Talon inhaled the sour stench of wood soaked in beer mixed with human perspiration. He had frequented enough shitty Third World dives in his Delta days to pick up on the undercurrent of violence when it was present. Some of the characters in this crowd were already visibly drunk, chasing vodka shots with beer and letting out shouts of anticipation while fist-pumping the air. Talon took a sip of his Rignes Pils, Norway's leading brew, and waited.

He didn't have to wait for long.

The lights soon dimmed and the bar grew silent. Even the hushed whispers ceased. The energy had changed — an air of reverence and dark wonder now permeated the establishment.

The stage lit up in a furious blaze of moody lights that speared through the pub's smoky darkness. Four tall, gaunt and long-haired figures stood revealed. The silence gave way to ecstatic howls.

The members of Ice God were decked out in leather trench coats and black pants complemented by motorcycle boots. Spiked gauntlets and belts encircled their wrists and waists. Each band member wore a rune around his neck on a string necklace. Corpse paint with black highlights covered their faces. They made Talon think of Goths on steroids, or a twisted version of KISS. But unlike the classic, playful '70s rock group, these sinister figures projected a worn, haunted quality and their blackened eyes glittered with contempt and hatred. Lost souls who had declared war against mainstream society.

Only item missing is the church-burning kit, Talon thought.

Talon scanned the stage. Still no sign of Rezok. The feverish anticipation in the pub was nearing its breaking point. Suddenly a raspy, grave-dark voice emanated from the darkness.

"Are you ready for the final winter?"

The question achieved its desired effect - the crowd went nuts. Rezok knew how to work up his flock, and they were eager for it. The power of the black-metal god could not be denied. As the band began to unleash the first volley of their sonic assault, the lights dimmed slightly in anticipation of the night's main attraction. The guitars rose to a furious crescendo as Rezok stepped onto the stage.

One glance told Talon the reports had been true. Ice God's lead singer didn't have to wear corpse paint to create a vampiric countenance; his complete absence of pigment appeared to be natural. Rezok was an albino, his skin and long flowing hair a pure white color. Like all those afflicted with this chromosomal abnormality, he had a heightened sensitivity to light. Defying the myths that had sprung up around albinism, his eyes weren't pink or red but a faded gray and burned with an intensity that electrified the room.

Talon remembered watching an interview where Rezok claimed that he buried his clothes before a performance so they would soak up the scent of the grave. The outlandish claims had elicited chuckles, but Talon wasn't laughing right now. Something about experiencing Ice God's lead singer up close made it impossible to ignore him. Rezok was a force to be reckoned with.

He brought up his mic and switched to Norwegian, barking another guttural greeting at his enraptured fans. Talon didn't understand the words, but he could gauge their effect on the crowd - Rezok was rallying an army.

Fighting in the war on terror had given Talon a healthy respect for the power of misguided ideology. It didn't matter whether it was a Jihadist preaching to a flock of extreme Islamists in some Saudi Arabian mosque or a Norwegian black-metal god addressing his followers in a Bergen dive.

The music kicked in. The shrieked vocals, demonic tempos and static-infused production built into a roar of angst, fury and loathing. Despite the noise and unfiltered aggression, Talon couldn't deny the undeniable power and evil beauty of the band's ferocious set.

Talon didn't judge people by the music they listened to. Hell, he'd followed his share of crazy bands over the years. Theatrics came with the gig. The edgier the band, the greater the appeal. But black metal seemed to be all about the edge and the abyss that lurked beyond.

As Ice God powered through the first couple of songs, the throng erupted in a blaze of violent movement. Rezok's leather-clad followers pumped their arms as if possessed. Elbows shot out wildly. Enthralled by the performance, no one cared who was hit or hurt during these drunken pub aerobics. Most of the fans welcomed the violent onslaught, cherishing each bruise and bloody nose as hard-earned, much-treasured battle scars.

One foolish fan tried to elbow Talon in the ribs.

Bad idea.

Talon anticipated the sly attack, sidestepped the blow and snatched the big man's right hand. He twisted the limb and the fan let out a pain-filled grunt. They traded glances and Talon's cold, hard stare made him back off.

You're not as dumb as you look, Talon thought.

As the concert wore on, somehow the message got around not to mess with the American and the other moshing fans maintained a respectful distance.

Talon continued to study the spectral figures, memorizing their movements. They all shared a lean, lanky quality he'd found among the best operators. The aggressive athleticism of their performance could not be denied. He'd have to factor their speed and stamina into any future encounters with them. If Simon Casca's intel was to be believed, two of the band members were once in the Marinejegerkommandoen, the Norwegian special forces. They'd been kicked out of the MJK after being accused of assault and rape. Talon wasn't going up against some soft, beer-bellied mama's boys with a penchant for pagan rock. These were elite soldiers gone bad.

All of a sudden, an overeager concertgoer jumped up on stage and whipped out a razorblade. The piece of sharp metal sparkled in the strobing spotlights.

Talon saw no fear in Rezok's eyes. Instead, his dead-white features lit up with an approving smile.

The fan raised both his hands and bowed as if he had indeed entered the presence of some Nordic god. Without hesitation, he drew the razor over his palm and held up his gushing hand at Rezok in a twisted salute. The abrupt movement sent speckles of blood flying across the stage. A few drops hit Rezok's face, the crimson in stark contrast with the marble of his skin.

What happened next stunned Talon. With a hungry smile, Rezok licked his lips until the enamel of his teeth turned scarlet with the other man's blood.

The occult assassin was beginning to understand how Rezok had earned his nickname.

FIND OUT ABOUT UPCOMING RELEASES, FREE BOOK GIVEAWAYS, EXCLUSIVE CONTENT AND GIFT CARD SWEEPSTAKES BY JOINING THE MAILING LIST. WHEN YOU SUBSCRIBE YOU ARE AUTOMATICALLY ENTERED INTO AN AMAZON GIFT CARD SWEEPSTAKES!

www.williammassa.com

If you enjoyed the story, please leave a review for others so they can discover the book too.

If you have notes, thoughts or comments about this book, feel free to email me at

williammassabooks@gmail.com

Writing can be a solitary pursuit but rewriting can be a group effort. I strive to make each book better than the last and feedback is incredibly helpful.

ABOUT THE AUTHOR

William Massa is a screenwriter, script consultant and book reviewer (http://horrornovelreviews.com/) He has lived in New York, Florida, Europe and now calls Los Angeles his home. William writes horror, thrillers, science fiction and dark fantasy. More books are on the way.

COVER ART/CREDITS

Vampire image © 2014 under license of istockphoto.

Cover Design by Jun Ares & William Massa

Proofing by John Evans.
thefictionfixer@gmail.com You're a rockstar!

OTHER NOVELS

FEAR THE LIGHT: WHO MURDERED DRACULA?

Over the centuries, many had tried to kill the Count. All had failed. Until now...

Eight vampires gather at Dracula's castle to solve his murder. But as the sun rises outside the chateau, a voice cries out and another creature of the night is slain. Trapped, the sun burning bright outside, the vampires realize they have met their match — a killer who plans on picking them off one by one!

As the daylight reigns and their numbers dwindle, a dark suspicion grows — could Dracula's murderer be hiding in plain sight?

GARGOYLE KNIGHT

When his kingdom is threatened by an ancient evil, a king is forced to make the ultimate sacrifice. If he is to defeat an army of monsters, he must become one himself! His victory carries a terrible   price...   An   eternity   frozen   in   stone.

Fifteen centuries later, the Celtic warrior is awakened when the world needs him most. A stranger in a strange land with his only guide a beautiful archeology student, he must battle his old adversary once again, all while struggling with his own darkness. For he is by day a man, by night cursed to become... The GARGOYLE!

CPSIA information can be obtained
at www.ICGtesting.com
Printed in the USA
LVOW04s1009281116
514733LV00031B/601/P